Copyright © 2019 Alfie Anfield

All rights reserved. The use of any part of this publication, reproduced, transmitted in any form or by any means electronic, mechanical, photocopying, recording or otherwise, or stored in a retrieval system without the prior written consent of the author – or in the case of photocopying or other reprographic copying, license from the Canadian Copyright Licensing Agency – is an infringement of the copyright law.

This book is sold subject to the condition that it shall not, by way of trade or otherwise be lent, re-sold, hired out or otherwise circulated without the author's prior consent in any form of binding or cover other than that in which it is published and without a similar condition including this condition being imposed on the subsequent purchase

This is a work of fiction. Names, characters, business, places, events, locales and incidents are either the products of the author's imagination or used in a fictitious manner. Any resemblance to actual persons, living or dead, or actual events is purely coincidental

MUST BE MERE FOLLY

Alfie Anfield

To my JP; my inspiration, my catalyst, my soulmate.

CHAPTER 1.

'It's not half bad is it?'

The boys for once agreed with Bert as they sat on the patio outside their restaurant looking down on the foot and bike path running alongside the new canal. It linked the lake with the main river. Only the brightly coloured special flat bottom boats were allowed on the canal. Operated by students, they transported people to the various landing and pick up stages, letting them on and off at the various access points to places of interest. Alongside the canal were walkways and bike paths enabling people to travel up and down the canal. This cut traffic and parking issues downtown and allowed people to travel east to west and vice versa quite quickly, with minimal obstruction and contention. The boys, as their eyes wandered along the canal, discussed the backdrop. The great attraction is that it gives you a whole different perspective on the city. It's like seeing it from the inside rather than driving through or past downtown with blinkers on. Notwithstanding the beauty and the practicality of the canal in summer; in winter it became a social space with skating and other winter activities centred around the frozen canal.

'Don't you feel a sense of relief at not only seeing what we have achieved but actually using the 'completed article' carried on Bert with a sense of pride.

As they sat watching people enjoying not only the restaurants, the cafes, the shops, the artisan workshops around them, they revelled in the fact that they were creating and providing Mere Folly with a stunning infrastructure and lifestyle. All of a sudden Mere Folly was on the map and was not only being appreciated by the locals but outsiders were visiting in droves.

'What kept you?' Bert looked up at Jim as he sat down. Did you leave your wallet with your wife?

'I didn't mention this as I was pissed off, but last week I was looking after my daughter's house while they were away on holiday. The people who collect the re cycling bags didn't pick up hers. They left it there with a sticker on it saying there was stuff in the bag that wasn't re cyclable. No mention of what it was, they just left the bag there. I took a careful look at what was in the bag, it looked good to me and couldn't find anything in there that shouldn't have been.'

'Were they having a bad day?'

'Who knows? Are you telling me that these guys check out all the bags they throw on their truck or is the city paying garbage gestapo to wander round checking the bags? I wouldn't have minded if they had put a note on the sticker explaining what was in there that shouldn't have been, we can all learn. So, I took the sticker off and left exactly the same bag with exactly the same contents out, Guess what? You're right, they took it this time.

'This is all bullshit and a waste of money; they change the rules month by month. I gave up some time ago and don't bother anymore.' Kev got out his phone and was soon chatting to the person in charge garbage collection and arranged a meeting for later that day.

'What was that all about?' asked Jim.

'He said he could fit me in in a couple of weeks. You heard my comment to that. He wasn't happy when I told him that I could fit him in at 5 pm.'

'Now I get it,' chuckled Jim, 'aren't the workers lining up to go home at about four fifteen? He's going to love you eating into his drinking time'

'Can't wait,' said Kev. 'I'll see if he has all the schedules, data and expense spread-sheets I asked him for.'

As they were finishing off their bottle of wine Tom noticed a couple ambling backwards and forwards, obviously looking for a table. 'We are just leaving; would you like this table.'

'We are? I've just got here' gulped Jim. Then he suddenly realized that while they were sat there, profit was being diminished as the couple would be paying for their wine and food.

"Nice guys,' the man smiled at the waiter gave them menus. 'They seem to like this place.'

'They should do' said the waiter, 'they own this place and most of the City'.

The couple sat looking at each other not knowing whether he was having them on and decided that he was having a laugh with them, obviously four harmless seniors out for a drink, the couple smiled at each other........

The boys walked along the canal and on to Chat where they sat at their table at the back of the restaurant. The table in the front corner by the big window, probably the best table in the place, was empty most of the time it. Customers asked for the table as they arrived but it always appeared to be booked, yet never used. The boys when in attendance would nod to the receptionist if they would like people to be seated there. The staff could never figure out who and why. The only person that they knew had to be seated there for certain was Councillor Moron.

'Well, well, well' laughed the boys, as the bottle of Amarone arrived. They weren't laughing at the bottle of wine rather at who should wander in and sit at the table but the moron and a guy they didn't know.

They quickly put their ear plugs in.

'I wonder who he is, anybody know him?' asked Tom.

They listened intently

As the couple talked, the boys became more and more interested. After a few minutes more of listening in, it became apparent that their relationship was rather more carnal than getting together for a brief business lunch, it didn't appear as if he was a business colleague or someone involved with her in her position as councillor.

As Jim put it, 'why would she bring him to Mere Folly? They could spend the night at his hotel. We know that she is dumber than two sets of hammers but she can't be this stupid. I wonder if anybody wandering in will say hello to her looking to be introduced. How will she handle that?'

'Why would she bring him in here, or for that matter take him anywhere in Mere Folly? asked Bert, everybody knows her here so what's her game?

'Consider this,' decided Kev, 'we are the only people who know that they are having it off. Anybody else would just take it for granted that they were discussing business.'

'You are right Kev, but we know what's going on and I don't get it' whispered Bert, he kept stating the obvious 'Why would she bring him here? Everybody knows her and everybody knows that that isn't her husband.'

Mary Moron was slightly chubby, but not unattractive. She was, in her own mind the successor, next time around to the Mayor of Mere Folly. Her reasoning was quite logical as she, not that she would agree with the terminology, was the Mayor's mistress. Mistress or not, they had been having an affair for years. How they had got away with it was anybody's guess. Her husband was out of town a lot and thought of his wife's venture into politics as a hobby. In his mind, it gave her something to save her from being bored while he was away. On the other hand, Mrs. Mayor was so concerned about maintaining her social standing she appeared oblivious to what Mr. Mayor was up to. As long as she was in a position to Lord herself over all and sundry, she was quite happy. It would never occur to her that the times he was off to out of town meetings or slipping away for a couple of hours in the afternoon or for a weekend he was bedding councillor Moron.

Bert was waiting for an answer to his question. Nothing was forthcoming which was unusual.

Then Tom, having been deep in thought awoke. 'Perhaps she wants someone to see her out and about and be noticed and even talked about'.

'I like it,' said Jim, 'it makes sense, her husband's never around, what can the Mayor do or say'.

Kev was deliberating. 'The Mayor probably knew nothing about her liaison. Was she waiting for him to wander in or the gossip reach him? Was she trying to intimidate him and show him that he needed her? Was she illustrating or even demonstrating that she didn't need him as she had other fish in the sea?'

From the conversation at the table it appeared that she had literally picked this guy up at a business function that he had been taken to by a client. They were reminiscing over their first meeting, and how it didn't take them long to get together in his hotel room. He had asked her to visit him, she said she would prefer it if they took it easy and suggested that they get together on his next visit. She didn't know that he immediately went and arranged a business trip out there. He would contact one of his two clients and offer to buy them lunch. The offer of a free lunch, went down well, they lapped it up. He had his alibi arranged and if anybody in the office asked, not that they would, his clients needed him for three or four days.

The boys were taking it in as Elliot was captivating the moron with his smooth chatter, they didn't know about the devious planning behind the scenes, but they heard enough to form a dislike for the guy and only knowing a quarter of the story that the moron was being shafted in more ways than one.

'What do you want to do next' she asked

'That's up to you, why not leave him?'

She told him she was always thinking about that, she got up, left the table and headed for the door. It took some time for Elliot to pay the bill, but when he eventually got out of the door, she was there waiting for him.

The boys were listening to all this as she left, still trying to figure out what she was doing and why choose her home base to meet. They couldn't understand it, why so serious? she's only known the guy five minutes. It didn't make sense

'Perhaps it is as Tom says, she does want someone to see her out and about and be noticed and even talked about' said Kev.

'Yeah,' Bert was not so sympathetic 'what a mess she's got herself into, she's got a husband and the Mayor in tow and now this clown. She's certainly material for the next mayor of Mere Folly.

'I know who he is,' said Tom. 'I helped him get the only three accounts he has. As soon as I retired and was of no use to him, what price loyalty? He's the kind of guy that once you out serve your usefulness to them, they drop you like a hot potato. However, so as not to be biased, let's see if others see him in the same light. Bert do you still have some contacts who can do a number on this guy and get the real nitty gritty background on him as soon as possible.'

A week later the boys were in Chat listening to Bert.

'Evidently he's a real door knob. My guy really had no problem digging up stuff and getting people to talk. He had clawed his way up the executive ladder, more by luck than judgement, being in the right place at the right time. A perfect example was how he ended up in his present position. The company he worked for being bought by an American conglomerate. His boss, who ran the place was a legend in the business, to the shock of everybody, figured he had had enough, didn't want to work for an American company and decided to retire.

The company panicked, its management wanted to keep some stability with its new acquisition both internally and its perception within the marketplace. Even they knew that Insurance was a people business and Monty had developed relationships as he built the company's national presence.

As Elliot was the only senior person with service and tenure, he was appointed to manage the combined operation. Of course, that went straight to his head and knowing how the Americans liked to hire and fire he decided to milk them through his expense account before his time with the company expired. He didn't know a lot about the technical side of the business, but once in a senior position, with knowledgeable staff around, he found out that with the art of management delegation he really didn't need to know much anyway. Elliot found out over the years the real knowledgeable technicians were rather shy and intimidated easily. He was six feet five inches tall, loud mouthed, to the extent that he was not afraid of being vulgar. He was good on his feet, didn't care who he intimidated consequently got away without being knowledgeable as he bullied and bullshitted his way through life. Presently single, he had been married previously and had the odd relationship or six, so with plenty of time on his hands, he lived literally on his expense account otherwise he would have been in dire-straights. Having to pay alimony and support his kids he still needed money, the chance and euphoria to make some easy money impacted his common sense. Being married with a couple of kids didn't seem to bother him, this was a means to an end. A lot of his income after supporting his ex-wife and kids was spent on building and protecting the image of a successful business person. The expensive clothes and trimmings; of course, all the other extras such as the lunches, dinners, hotels, business class air fares and of course the golf club membership, were picked up, one way or another, through his employer.

His colleagues in the business would often joke amongst themselves that he thought with his dick and if he had a brain, he would be dangerous. He buffooned his way through life with a bunch of his colleagues on their drunken business fishing and golf trips. The fishing trip for his buddies was the highlight of his year. He didn't have that many clients, so to fill up the roster he had to ask around a bit and eventually the twelve would meet at a five-star hotel on the west coast for a weekend of meals and booze prior to getting on the private plane. There was a game of golf thrown in and a trip to a local strip club all in the name of making sure that his 'business friends' had a good time.

He was disliked by most of the people he worked with and around his business fraternity. It was amazing once you got going with people in his circle, because they didn't like him how they opened up. One employee who got to hear of the monkeyshines put it to his colleagues, 'I can't get a pay rise to support my family yet these clowns are allowed to waste all that money having a good time and drink and eat their brains out. Hard to believe that these are the so-called executives in the insurance world who demand us to work hard and respect them. While they all get drunk, having a good time on the tab of the company then come back and tell us that times are tough and benefits and pay have to be frozen. To many of Elliot's industry associates and the wider band of the rumour mill it wouldn't surprise them with what he was up to as he always came across as having a slimy personality; in fact, he was a bit of a joke and his reputation as a coarse sex mad deposit of filth went before him.'

'My investigator's words, not mine, said Bert.

'He really appears to be a bit of a slime ball' doesn't he?' said Jim 'we should phone the mayor and tell him what his friendly moron is involved with.

Tom panicked, 'No, that's their problem, we haven't got where we are by getting involved in the Mayor's and the moron's sex life, let's just stick to plan A, watch it evolve and take advantage.'

'This guy Elliot intrigues me,' added Bert.

'Me to,' said Kev. 'You guys were involved in the insurance business; don't you know him or of him.'

'You are a pratt,' Bert said, 'that's like saying to you, because you laid an underground pipe here do you know the guy who dug a hole five thousand miles away.'

Tom was still concerned though. 'I know what he's like and can't figure out is why the moron is having an affair with him on her own patch. It won't matter to him, he does that kind of stuff for a living, but the councillor hasn't got a clue about his life she thinks he is a straight up and down business man.'

'Wait a minute though, people don't know that they are having an affair, the perception is that they are meeting on business. If they nip off to his hotel fifteen clicks away, nobody will know.'

'Mr. Mayor, how are you?' asked Jim as the Mayor arrived and sat down at their table. The earbuds were quickly put away. 'What can we do for you this fine day.'

'So, what are you reprobates up to.'

'Actually, we were just wondering who the councillor's new boy-friend was.'

Trust Jim thought the boys collectively under their breath. Didn't we just say that we wouldn't get involved Kev thought as he rolled his eyes at the others.

'That's typical of you low life's, she filled me in. She met him at a function and she feels that he can help the city risk manager with our insurance.'

'Oh, that's his ploy.' As Jim needled the Mayor.

'What's that supposed to mean.'

'Nothing' said Tom, interrupting as Bert kicked Jim under the table.

He sensed that the Mayor could get a bit bent out of shape. 'What do you know about him, I am sure that you have done your due diligence especially if you are going to do business with him.'

The mayor looked rather sheepish, 'well the councillor seems pretty keen on him.'

'Stone me,' laughed Bert. 'You still haven't got it through your head yet that due diligence isn't a matter of getting your councillor to have sex with the candidate.'

You really are sick,' said the Mayor as he got up, 'I've got to go to the washroom.'

'Maybe,' added Bert, 'maybe we should tell him what we know. What harm can it do.'

'A lot', said Tom 'we shouldn't get involved we have a lot on our plate, let's see if he can sort his own mess out.'

'Hold on, hold on,' said Jim, 'What if he screws up. Think about it, we have got where we have got by controlling the Mayor, not letting him loose.'

'Jim's right said Bert, let's keep him in our pocket'

'What pocket,' said the Mayor as he sat down again. 'Oh Nothing,' said Tom, 'we were concerned about the councillor's buddy and decided to check him out.'

'What, while I was in the washroom.'

'No,' said Bert. 'We saw them together in here and wondered who he was.'

'Nothing gets by you guys does it?'

'Hopefully not,' said Kev, 'if we left it to you, we could be in big trouble, so here's the scoop'.

The Mayor was staggered as Bert filled him in.

'How did she get involved with him?'

'Easy.' Said Tom. 'He's a slime ball looking for a way to pick up some business from the City, she happened to be at the function, what better way than to use a councillor to get in and have a bit of nookie at the same time. He probably couldn't believe his luck.'

The boys could see the Mayor seething.

'She's doing this behind my back.'

Jim cracked up. 'So, what are you doing behind your wife's back

'That's different.'

Jim cracked up again. 'what's different

She's up to something,' said Bert. 'again, why would she not hide the fact that she was having a bit of the other and flaunt this guy all over town. She's having a go at you Mr Mayor she wants to make you mad; she wants you to punt her.'

'She couldn't do that I have too much on her.'

'Think how much I have on her,' said the Mayor, 'for instance, the meters. She would end up in jail.'

'You idiot,' said Tom. 'You have a lot on her, she has a lot on you. She knows damn well that neither of you can say anything you'll both be ruined. You should just lay back, let her get on with her toy boy while you wait for the chance.'

'Tom's right' said Bert, 'Keep on chasing her to have sex. That's not what she wants. When you are humping her, she will be pissed off while you are enjoying yourself and knowing you are pissing her off and getting revenge'

'Gentlemen you are geniuses, I can now sleep at night'.

'Depends who you happen to be in bed with,' laughed Kev.

Sat on the patio alongside the canal on a warm clear evening Kev was looking into his beer, 'I was thinking about you guys.'

'That's very noble of you,' Jim said smiling at two ladies walking along the canal footpath.

'Seriously, you know a bit about insurance, the City and its residents pay a chunk of money for insurance and we have a guy who thinks Mere Folly's insurance business is worth using one of the councillors to get it. Why don't we start our own insurance company and use it to insure ourselves and give citizens cheap insurance?

'Great idea Kev but it takes lots of money to capitalize an insurance company.'

Tom was quiet, then out of nowhere, 'there might be a way. Perhaps we could use a limited amount of capital and use our good friend Elliot, although he doesn't know that he is a friend yet and reinsure everything to death.

The boys thought an insurance company warranted some thought. 'Just think,' said Bert, 'we could set up a resident insurance scheme. Automobile, home, personal a mandatory program. There are lots of people living in Mere Folly with insurance expertise, we would be creating employment for the residents. They would love to pop down the road to go to work instead of making the trek that many of them do.

Three days later the boys were meeting with their lawyers, accountants and the Government regulators in Mere Folly. The regulators couldn't believe what they were hearing.

'You are actually serious about this,' said the deputy minister.

'Listen,' said Tom, 'your time and especially our time is important. You know what we have done to Mere Folly, this will be our next project.'

The regulators were bemused and started laughing.

'Gentlemen,' said Peter, one of the lawyers. 'I don't know if you realise who you are meeting with. I understand that you know three of these people and their insurance expertise, however, what you obviously don't know is that they are totally responsible for putting Mere Folly on the map.'

Peter then gave each of the bureaucrats a précis of what they had done and their holdings. 'Now once you have digested this we would like to get down to business.'

Bert winked at Peter acknowledging a job well done.

All of a sudden, the bureaucratic arrogance had gone,

The boys took over and explained what they had in mind. They would present a business plan as soon as possible to take their venture a step further.

The deputy minister was impressed and went on to say that he would encourage this project, but the boys could tell that the career bureaucrats, weren't as convinced. A project such as this would mean a lot of work and the chance that their lack of expertise would be noticed.

As a parting shot, Tom explained that the beauty of having a new local insurer, operating a City mandatory insurance program would have an additional bonus. It would take away the power of the Insurance Council. The Council as everyone who dealt with it and its archaic approach to licensing was run by people that couldn't make it in the insurance business. The insurance company would be run by, managed and operated by experienced insurance people with expertise gained over many years.

For once, the regulators smiled as there was no love lost between them and the Council. Tom went on to describe how anybody can get a broker / agent's licence with a couple of days studying and after a few more weeks have authority over people with years of insurance management and underwriting experience. This really caught their attention. He went on to say how absurd it was that an employee of an insurance company with twenty-five years management and or underwriting experience with a level one licence theoretically would have to get approval from a nineteen-year-old with three weeks experience and a level two licence. The new company would not be forcing its staff to be licensed. Hiring criteria would be strictly based upon experience and expertise.

The deputy minister asked where the business was going to come from.

Bert jumped in, 'the base will be Mere Folly's business and a mandatory residents' insurance scheme,'

You can't do that,' said one of the bureaucrats.

Why not,' said Bert, there are a number of mandatory government programs dotted about the country.

'But you are not the Government.'

'What does that matter? Mere Folly was a democracy the last time I looked, the council operates the City for the benefit of its citizens and what we are proposing, no, going to do will benefit its citizens.

Then Tom joined in. 'We will also deal with local brokers. These guys are eternally frustrated by lack of service from the big global insurers. With London and domestic brokers and underwriters spending half their time drinking inside or outside a pub, clients can't get decisions or answers to their questions or submissions. Our brokers will be happy feeding us the good stuff and will willingly give to a local insurer willing to provide local expertise and service. As our market provides brokers with the service and expertise they crave, they will send the crap out of the country.

'Goodness, I didn't realise,' said the deputy minister, as usual completely ignorant of his own portfolio. 'I hope this works; I must admit I am looking forward to reading your plan and taking in some of your ideas.'

After they had bid farewell to the entourage, Bert looked at the other three and shook his head; did you hear that Deputy Minister? "I didn't realise", 'that's an indictment of how little they know of what's actually going on and how useless those bureaucrats are. Was it Henry II who said "will no one rid me of this meddlesome priest." That's how I feel about this Government, the sooner we are free from them the better.'

CHAPTER 2.

In Mere Folly cannabis could only be consumed in a person's residence. The definition of residence excluded yard or garden, with one concession; outbuildings, maximum size 120 square feet, these were classed as a residence. This was a bone of contention with the politicians and lawmakers who put the law into place, but the silent majority won through in the end. They would have preferred the law didn't exist in the first place, especially the effect it have on children growing up around it. However, after months of bartering decided not to rock the boat any further as the powers that be were hinting that consequences could follow.

The Mayor was still having a go at the lawmakers, he gained a certain amount of notoriety with his plea, 'What about our children?'

'It will only affect those children of idiotic parents, stupid enough to consume cannabis around them,' was the answer he received. Followed by, 'As long as parents don't smoke cannabis around children. Well, some parents still smoke tobacco around their kids, so what difference does it make, tobacco or cannabis.'

'I won't even stoop that low with an answer,' said the Mayor.

The odd shed started springing up in gardens, they became known as pot sheds as distinct to potting sheds.

As if the Mayor hadn't got enough on his plate, he was being savaged by Mrs. Mayor who was distinctly paranoid that her husband had not managed to get his hands on one of the penthouse suites in the Vineyard condo. He probably could have had any one of the remaining condo units, but there were only four penthouse suites and they were taken by the boys.

It was Kev who laughed, 'We dodged a bullet there, guys. Imagine having those two as neighbours, it's bad enough having you three, it would been a nightmare. On second thoughts Tom why don't you give yours to Mr. and Mrs. Mayor, after all its big and you live in it by yourself.'

The other three looked incredulously at Kev.

'Only joking,' he smiled.

Mr. Mayor tried to explain the situation, but to no avail, Mrs Mayor wasn't too pleased, 'we could have any other unit in the building.' he said.

' Another unit!' she shouted. "The wife of the Mayor in one of the lesser units, are you out of your mind, how could I face my social circle and the public of Mere Folly.'

'I've made up my mind'.

Oh no thought the mayor, what now. What he did know was that it was going to cost him money and probably lots of it.

'We are going to have this house renovated from top to bottom.'

'Are you stupid woman, have you any idea how much that is going to cost?'

'I don't care,' said Mrs. Mayor, 'you owe me, you had the chance to put me where I belong in this city, in the penthouse. But you are so weak, you couldn't do it, so we will renovate this house to the standard that a person of my standing should have.'

The Mayor was mortified, but if he wanted an easy and comfortable life then he had to obey herself.

The next day the Mayor was on the phone to his friendly builder and a couple of other contractors to whom he had given city funded jobs. Now was the time to call back his favours. He arranged for a friendly architect, again, calling in another favour, to meet with his wife to discuss the preliminary scope of the renovation.

Unfortunately for the Mayor, the meeting lasted less than thirty minutes,

'She's a fruit loop,' the architect cried to the Mayor, which didn't surprise him, he already knew that the architect would be up against it but thought he would have lasted longer than he did.

Mrs, Mayor told the Mayor in no uncertain terms that she needed someone who could actually relate to her feel for beauty, architectural prominence and culture.

This presented the Mayor with a problem, where could he find an architect and or designer who could work with and deliver Mrs. Mayor's concept, however bizarre that might be. Even after many years of earning favours from corruption, the Mayor eventually started to run out of 'friends', nobody fancied working for Mrs. Mayor. She was single handily destroying the network of corruption that the Mayor built over many years in a matter of weeks.

The Mayor was beside himself, having now literally run out of favours. He was wondering how he was going to pay for this monumental renovation, when Mrs. Mayor walked into his office.

Not thinking, 'Oh, it's you,' slipped out of his mouth.

Normally he would have been lambasted, but today Mrs. Mayor was in a happy go lucky mood and she was smiling, which was a clue that Mr. Mayor picked up on and was immediately nervous.

'Thank goodness there is somebody around here that can make things happen.'

The Mayor knew, he was in trouble.

'I have solved the problem of who will design and build our new house.'

'Just how are you going to do that,' laughed the Mayor 'and who might that be?' said a concerned Mr. Mayor.' You don't know anybody in the home building industry or for that matter, designers or architects.'

That's where you are wrong,' said Mrs. Mayor arrogantly.

'It was staring us in the face. I have been talking to Mrs. Smith, she agreed to ask Charley to do the renovation and will help me to design it.

'Isn't that wonderful? I decided that as you weren't making any progress with the renovation, I would take over. I have had preliminary chats and discussions with Mrs. Smith. We are going to design and Charley Smith is going to do the work.'

The Mayor nearly choked. 'What the bloody hell do you pair of bozos' know about design and architecture?'

'Too bad,' said Mrs. Mayor as she left the Mayor to stew. 'I am off to meet her now to get the ball rolling. By the way, I assured Mrs. Smith that I would personally see to it that Charley would get lots of work as the City's construction projects moved along to pay for what they are doing for us.'

Mr. Mayor was unbelieving, he got up, walked round and kicked the couch.'

Limping back to his chair, 'dumb fuckin idiot' he yelled.

His mind was racing, of course she's too dumb and egotistical to realise and understand that I don't control those City projects anymore. She doesn't get the fact that you need money for these jobs and lots of it. Where does she think it's coming from, as always, she just goes out and spends without consequence? Then the light went on as it dawned on him and gave him some comfort that the concern he had over where the money was coming from had disappeared. He felt better, he was at peace, his mind was clear as he thought to himself why not let her get on with it. Any screw ups would be her fault and of course the Smiths would be doing the work for nothing. It would be years before Charley realised that he wouldn't be getting any backhanders in return. He could also tell him that he could use, as advertising, the fact that he was doing and or did the building, design and renovation work on the Mayor's house. Mind you down the road that probably wouldn't do him a lot of good though, as once his wife and Mrs. Smith had finished with the place, it would be a piece of junk anyway and people would be laughing at it.

All of a sudden, he was feeling much better, in fact he was going to encourage his wife to move along as quickly as possible.

Mrs. Mayor couldn't understand the Mayor's change in attitude. All of a sudden, he was encouraging her. She didn't realise he was enjoying putting the noose around her neck. It also meant that she was out of his hair and he could concentrate on other things, especially Mary Moron.

After dinner that night it suddenly occurred to him again. 'So where are we going to live while you are knocking this place about.'

'Oh, didn't I tell you!'

'Tell me what?'

'That nice Mrs. Smith has a nice little condo that Charley has just finished renovating. She told me that we can borrow it until we can move into our completed house.'

'So how much will that cost us.'

'Nothing,' said a startled Mrs. Mayor. 'You don't understand it do you, people know who I am and as the leading lady in Mere Folly they want to be and need to be associated with me. She is already out there bragging that her and her husband have been chosen and have the honour of renovating the Mayor's house.'

The Mayor felt like vomiting, but he had learnt over the past few years of mixing with the boys that life is for living, keep the wife happy and you can more or less do your own thing. This suited him right down to the ground.

Plans were completed and the demolition scheduled in preparation for the renovation of the pink palace. Then he looked at the plans and couldn't believe his eyes.

'Where's the garden gone?'

'The new kitchen has been extended slightly,' she said

'Slightly, it's taken over the bloody garden. How much is that going to cost? and look at this why do we need five bathrooms, there's only two of us.'

'You don't get it do you,' she went on, 'I know that we only have four bedrooms, but we need a spare for when important people come to visit.'

The Mayor and Mrs. Mayor moved into the condo. He still couldn't understand why they needed five bathrooms and a kitchen the size of a basketball court, but he heeded his latest philosophy, 'while stupidity reigns have fun'.

The boys sat in Chat with the Mayor, he filled them in on his residential saga. They had heard snippets while eavesdropping in on Mrs. Mayor and Mrs. Smith as they discussed their plans for the house. Now was the time to hear the Mayor's version. Obviously, they didn't tell him that they had a rough idea of what was going on. Listening to Mrs. Mayor and Mrs. Smith was illuminating to say the least.

'Mr. Mayor,' said Tom, 'what are they really going to do to your house?'

'I haven't a clue, all I know is that we are going to have five bathrooms.'

'But there are only two of you,' laughed Bert.

'That's exactly what I said,' spluttered the Mayor, 'but it's like talking to a brick wall. If she doesn't get her way then she just sulks. She has no idea about the economics of anything.

'You mean to say that you haven't seen the finished article's drawings?'

'No,' said the Mayor, 'and I don't really care.'

'What's this costing you, it must be an arm and a leg. You'd have been better off buying one of our condo's,' jumped in Jim.

'I agree. But it's all your fault.'

'How come?'

'If we could have had a penthouse, she would have gone for that, but you only built four.'

'There are lots more units in the building,' Jim went on.

'Aah but not penthouse suites. Don't forget that the Mayor's wife has to be seen to be living in the best spot in town and that is a penthouse suite, not a lower unit in a condo.'

'She's a bloody snob,' said Bert, 'how do you put up with her all the time? Stupid question, you don't, you have two women so you can escape when you need to.'

'I suppose you are right,' said a dismayed Mayor, 'but you don't have to live and put up with the wife, I have to go home to her, she's insufferable.'

'So again,' said a frustrated Jim, 'how much is this reno costing?'

'I don't know,' said the Mayor.

'You have to have some idea, you clown.' said Kev.

'Mrs. Smith is helping her design the thing and Charley Smith is building it.'

'But she's not a designer,' smirked Kev.

'Nor is my wife and Charley certainly isn't that good a builder, so it will be a disaster'.

Tom looked puzzled. 'You don't seem that bothered.'

'I've learnt a lot from you guys, what's the worst that can happen, I know it will be a disaster. After a time, she will want to move because she will hear on the grape vine that it is ugly and she will be the laughing stock of the City.

'So, come on, how much?' went on Kev.

'For the tenth time, I haven't a clue and I really don't care.'

Kev wasn't going to let the Mayor rest. 'But who's paying the bills?'.

'The Smiths.'

Then the light came on. 'You crafty bastard,' said Bert. 'I get it; so, they help design, he builds and pays for the materials and then gets free advertising in that he has built the Mayor's house. Then expects that down the road you will give him City construction jobs, for which he can charge exorbitant amounts of money. You really are a crafty bastard, cunning as well, but you have one problem, you don't control City construction anymore.'

'I know,' smiled the Mayor. 'Another thing, I learnt off you guys, if he is dumb enough to do the renovations without getting paid for them, that's his problem. The longer he waits for the benefits to arrive the bigger the lesson he is going to learn. I never did like the guy anyway, he shafted the City enough times, made a fortune and now he is going to pay for it.'

'What happens if he comes after you for the money'

'I have enough on him, that he won't. Besides that, it is my wife who befriended them, who wanted to do the reno, and my wife who orchestrated this whole thing, so she can conduct the symphony.'

'You know Mr. Mayor, when I first met you,' said a humble Jim, 'I thought that you were an arsehole, but as time has moved on, I have learnt that even though you are still an arsehole I have learnt to tolerate you.'

'From you Jim, that's a compliment,' said the Mayor getting out of his chair. Shaking hands with the boys, he left.

'You know,' said Tom 'he could be in trouble if down the road Smith does go after him. He doesn't seem to care though, does he?'

'If he is sued, we should pay his bills for the title to his house.'

'Imagine,' jumped in Jim,' bailing him out, owning the Mayor's house and letting him carry on living in it for a nominal rent to cover our costs. I like it. Nobody would know, he wouldn't suffer any back stabbing or embarrassment.'

Kev, no fan of the Mayor would love it if he was humiliated and ground into the dirt. 'You have to be joking, that is going to be the ugliest monstrosity, it will be a real blot on the landscape.'

'Doesn't matter,' said Bert. 'Tom and Jim are right; we would have the Mayor really in our pocket. Think about it Kev, I know you can't stand the guy, but traits don't enter into this, you will have your revenge, knowing that he will beholden to us. Anyway, that's an inkling on our part which is a bit far-fetched and some way down the road.

CHAPTER 3

Lying in bed, Mary Moron extricated herself from the Mayor's legs and arms and sat upright with her back against the bedhead. 'I thought you would have commented on the Prime Minister coming to visit Mere Folly.'

'How could I think of him during sex, he would have put me right off.'

'I don't know whether that's a compliment or not,' she said, 'anyway why is he coming here? He never fills me with enthusiasm, we will all have to dress up and suck up to those bureaucratic idiots. However, it will put the City on the map. Of course, you wouldn't be enthused anyway, I was forgetting the main reason that you aren't too fond of him. It was his party that wouldn't nominate you to stand for them in the last election.'

'Alright, alright' said the Mayor, 'you will never let me forget that will you.'

Mary Moron went on; 'it doesn't matter now, but if it will make you happy, we should be able to milk his visit and take advantage.'

"What's he coming here for anyway? That's what I would like to know.'

'Well I presume he's upset at our stand against his cannabis law, but from what I hear, the official reason for the visit is that he wants to see what we have done to the City.'

'What do you mean? What we have done.

'Well you and I' said the Moron.

31

The Mayor was quiet, he was thinking to himself that he had two women in his life and they were both arrogant idiots. How did I deserve them?

Next day, in a hastily organised brainstorming meeting, the Mayor led the council in a pre-planning session on the PM's visit.

A couple of days later, after a lot of toing and froing with the PM's people, it was ordained that he would do a walk about and as a person of the people, attend a mini dinner in the Mayor's garden. This would give the impression that the PM was a man of the people. The bureaucrat soon corrected himself as he explained that the PM liked to mingle with everybody and wanted to be seen as one of the girls and boys. Quickly digressing, he went on to explain that a package would be forthcoming explaining how the visit would be organised, unfold and what the powers that be would expect from the people of Mere Folly. It hadn't occurred to the Mayor though that he wouldn't have a house, let alone a garden.

Mrs. Mayor was in seventh heaven. 'Imagine" she sighed, 'at last I will be able to mix with people of my own class. The Prime Minister and Mrs. Prime Minister dining at my house. We must get ready with the preparation; I will of course head up the committee. When is it?'

'In two weeks.' said the Mayor.

'Two weeks,' shrieked herself, 'two weeks you idiot, you'll have to get the date changed.'

'I can't do that,' said the Mayor, 'why?'

'You idiot,' she yelled at him re-emphasising the idiot.' They start work renovating tomorrow.'

'Well get them to postpone it,' he yelled back.

'Have you looked at the garden lately you dumb idiot, the builders have been preparing for a couple of days now. Look at that equipment out there, look at the materials out there, look at the hole out there, look at the mess out there.'

'How could you do this to me,' said Mrs. Mayor overcome with emotion.

'I didn't plan this,' he yelled back.

Next day Mrs. Mayor invited herself to the first meeting of the PM visit committee.

'What's she doing here?' said one of the councilors to Mary Moron.

'Who knows, she thinks she runs the place anyway so I suppose she figured she should be here to take over.'

'Well she runs the Mayor,' said Councilor Branch.

Mary Moron didn't say anything, if people knew who was really running the City, they would be shocked, so would the Mayor's wife she thought.

That evening, Mrs. Mayor was trying to get hold of her husband. Unfortunately, he was somewhat tied up on council business with Mary Moron.

As they lay in bed together, councilor Moron with her breasts right in the Mayor's eye line said that she should entertain the PM in her garden.

'I think that that's a great idea my love,' added the Mayor.

'Good,' said the Moron, I will start planning and making sure that my house and garden are spruced up to fit the occasion'. She was thrilled, not only was her house being used for the biggest event in Mere Folly history but the City would be picking up the tab. Then in the back of her mind she wondered how the Mayor was going to explain what would be happening. She was thrilled thinking how Mrs. Mayor would cope with that. Tomorrow though she would have designers and landscapers in to plan her 'spruce up.'

Mr. Mayor told the councilors by e mail that Mary Moron would be hosting the function. This really antagonized them, not only the fact that he hadn't the balls to address the councilors in person and used e mail which was bad enough. The big bombshell was that Mary Moron was going to host.

It wasn't so straightforward at his temporary home. Mrs. Mayor was even more cantankerous for obvious reasons, well to her anyway. Her shot at cementing her position as the leading socialite of Mere Folly by hosting the function the like of Mere Folly would never see again was gone.

'How can she be expected to put on and host such an event.' She complained to the Mayor.

'You will be helping to organize and will be there to help,' the Mayor trying his hardest to patronize and appease her so that he didn't have to keep on listening to her bitching for the next few weeks.

'Helping!' she screamed, 'I will be there to lead and be the City's eminent person and person of prominence.'

It was a blue-sky warm day, the boys sat at the side of the canal having a beer. As usual the canal was bustling with locals, visitors and tourists. Of course, not everybody was concerned about the PM's visit.

The Mayor, still pissed off after the party snubbed him as a candidate in the next Federal election, stressed to the council that they had made the decision to adapt the new cannabis law to suit the citizens of Mere Folly. They were not going to be intimidated by the pompous visitor. For once the members of council were in unison. However much the Government pushed, the Mere Folly council would push back

The day arrived, the Government entourage and the PM made the usual sanctimonious speeches in the council amber. They paid the traditional compliments to the city of Mere Folly, its vision and beauty.

The PM's assistant suggested that the PM and the Mayor meet to discuss the cannabis law behind closed doors. A couple of years ago the Mayor would have been an advocate of the PM but times, attitude and viewpoint had changed. He knew what would happen if he ended up alone in a private room with the PM and his cronies. He was not going to be railroaded and bullied.

The Mayor reminded the PM that as far as he was aware Mere Folly was a democracy and that all members of council should be able to listen to what the PM had to say.

This went down like a lead balloon. The lines had been drawn in the sand and the PM became more like his old self, the spoiled brat. Gone was the diplomacy and bullshit. This was his legacy, nobody especially some small-town dipstick was going to disrupt it. He stressed that the cannabis law was in force and that there was no turning back or bending the law by some small hic town in the middle of nowhere.

The mayor looked away from the PM's stare, he could sense that the arrogant prick wasn't used to being treated in this way.

'You know that you and Mere Folly are going to pay for this down the road, don't you?'

That was a stupid thing to say and if he did have the odd loyal supporter in Mere Folly, it also alienated them, the council and the rest of the populous. It was bad enough when word got out locally, which didn't take too long, but once the word got out across the nation all hell broke loose.

The PM, wishing it would rain or snow or there could be some form of pestilence so he could get out of this god forsaken hole.

However, it was a beautiful sunny and warm evening. He was persuaded to stay and see out the visit, his mind racing as he tried to figure out how he could get revenge. The retinue was escorted to councillor Moron's residence where an elaborate, for Mere Folly anyway, garden party had been set up.

After the gaffe by the PM with his threat to the council and the populous of Mere Folly, his people made it clear to him that he was in damage control. The speeches were patronising and pleasant, invitees mingled with the PM's people and a feeling of togetherness ensued. The PM was hating every minute of it.

As the evening settled in and the ambiance was helped by the amount of booze consumed, the smell of cannabis became more noticeable. Some of the PM's associates took the opportunity to light up 'joints' provided by the hosts. Invitees from Mere Folly and council members of course ignored the weed. The PM couldn't ignore the opportunity offered to him, he figured that it was a way to parade his law front and centre. As he puffed on his joint, from the bushes, a number of photographs were being taken, a phone call made and through the back gate of the garden a couple of senior Mere Folly police officers arrived.

Initially nobody thought that this was too strange, perhaps a coincidence bearing in mind the security required at such an event.

The police officers walked to the PM who was in the process of taking a puff of a cannabis joint and asked him whether that was cannabis that he was smoking.

'Of course, it is, you clowns, you haven't a clue, have you.' As he really wanted to stick it to the locals that his legacy was now law and he really didn't care whether they liked it or not that he was the PM and what he says goes. He was now having a great time sticking it to the locals.

'Join me,' he said to one of the officers, 'you are ok, it's now legal, you can tell your grand-kids that you smoked a joint with the Prime Minister,'

'Perhaps so in your garden,' but not in a garden in Mere Folly said the officer.

Immediately the PM's security detail surrounded him.

'You lot can come to headquarters as well if you like'

Next morning the whole country was in uproar, not angry, but laughing. The PM had threatened a city council and then been arrested for smoking cannabis in a residential garden. Government officials and lawyers were flown out to not only sort out the mess but also to keep a lid on what was happening.

The Mere Folly council met and voted unanimously to back the City police force.

The boys laughed as their newspaper proclaimed the fact that the PM would be standing trial in Mere Folly. Over a beer in Chat they couldn't believe it that the Mayor, the council and especially the police would have the balls to stand up to the Government.

'Just doing their job,' said Tom.

'If they hadn't then there would have been all hell to play and our paper would have absolutely milked it' added Bert.

Meanwhile, Mary Moron was still in a state of shock. She hadn't a clue what was happening. Her social event of the year and one chance to shine not only locally but also nationally, coming to an abrupt and utter halt. As she sat alone and deserted in the council chamber. she felt very much alone with the bottom having dropped out of her bucket.

However, across the City, Mrs Mayor was holding court in a coffee shop with a bunch of her stooges.

'Can you believe what happened last night,' she snickered. 'It just goes to show what happens if you leave an occasion like that to an amateur, that would never had happened if I had of been hosting the soiree. That poor PM, taken away to jail. Wait till I talk to Mr. Mayor about it, he wouldn't have dared let that happen if it had been in my garden. Why the Mayor would let that woman handle it I don't know. I bet he hardly knows her attributes and certainly wouldn't have any idea of her accomplishments and abilities. Knowing my husband, he probably did it on purpose to emphasise to the residents what happens if you don't know who you are dealing with and don't use quality.'

'Boy, your idea worked a treat said the Mayor.'

'Now you have to see it through,' said Kev.

'We will,' said a strangely contrite and sincere Mayor standing up. 'At first, I was rather nervous as already there are journalists and tv crews camped out in the City, but I am now finding it stimulating. Mere Folly is really on the map. You guys are right, what a way to bring people into the city without paying for advertising.'

As the mayor headed for the door, a party of suits walked in. Jim caught the eye of the hostess, who of course got the message. They were shown to THE table.

'Good thinking Jim, initially I thought that you were bored with us,' laughed Bert

'Don't recognise them, definitely not from here, must be worth the gamble.'

The Government lawyers were not very happy, having had to drop what they were doing and fly out to this hic town.

With the suits sat around THE table the boys waited and wondered. They were surprised as the compliments flew. Walking to Chat they walked along the canal and expressed their love of the downtown they thought it to be a real cute place.

'The only thing lacking is a decent hotel; I even hear that the place has a vineyard and some neat restaurants.' Ben was smiling, 'I mean look at this place, it could be our local.'

'Sounds like us thirty years ago,' grinned Tom, 'I wonder who they are and what they do.'

Tom looked through the line of tables, 'You know they all look the same. Dark suits white shirts, solid ties, they must be Americans.'

'Why would Americans be here in Mere Folly, I reckon they are media,' said Kev.

'Look at them most media people wouldn't dress the same and look like an advert for a morgue,' Jim sneered and suddenly put his finger to his lips

"I suppose that we had better fathom a way to get the idiot out of yet another mess. Any ideas?' One of the suits with glasses perched on the end of his nose was looking earnestly at his colleagues.

The boys were all attention trying to understand where the suits were coming from, it was getting clearer by the minute though.

The voice over the bug was clear. 'Really who gives a shit about the arrogant prick, but the Government never questions our bills.'

The boys could see the suit with glasses looking around to make sure that no one was eavesdropping.

'At least the money keeps rolling in so let's drink to the prick and his Government. It's not going to be easy to get him off this latest rap though, the PR people are struggling as well. Whilst he is paying us and picking up this tab, we have to work hard to get him off.' He waived at the waitress for another round.

'Government Lawyers,' said Jim.

'Government bastards' snarled Bert 'and I was beginning to like them.'

'C'mon' laughed Tom, 'they are only doing their job. In a roundabout way I like and admire them. The Government presents them with an opportunity, and makes it easy for them to take advantage. Let's face it's an opportunistic society that we live in and there are many out there who have, or are already taking advantage of the benefits provided by the Government. Here's to the poor taxpayer who has to support this corruption and excess.

Bert had his eyes to the ceiling, which meant that he was thinking. 'We should try and get some Government contracts, there's some easy money there.'

Kev jumped in straight away,' Haven't we got enough on our plate.'

'Yes, but its easy money,' reiterated Bert.

'Why wouldn't we,' said Jim.

'Jim, Bert, think about it went on Kev, 'Why would we want to get involved with the Government. With all that we do and are involved, there could be questions and involvement, no I am happy with guys like that staying at that end of the room and us down here.'

The PM had been given bail and whisked back to the capital. He was grilled in parliament. He was not a happy camper. Whatever, wherever, whenever he was going to have his revenge on Mere Folly. The PM, was committing political suicide as he announced that a new federal sales tax would be introduced strictly for Mere Folly. If the PM still had a few supporters, they were dissolving pretty quickly as citizens across the country were seeing him for what he was worth, an immature, petulant arrogant piece of work. With the election a year or so away, the PM had really created discontent, polls were suggesting that not only would he get hammered in an election, he would lose his seat and his party would be wiped out as well. The powers that be that pulled his strings were fearful.

Not all was joy and festivity in Mere Folly either, the citizens were besides themselves wondering what stunt the idiot in the ivory towers was going to pull next. Nevertheless, despite the punitive sales tax visitors and tourists were still flocking to see the city.

The boys listened intently as the lawyers discussed the legalities of how and whether they could get the case thrown out of court.

The lawyers were now even more convinced that the only way out for the PM was to prove that he was set up. Sat there, listening intently and not saying much at all was a young man, who appeared to be hardly out of school. He suddenly cut in.

'If it works great, but have you given it some thought as to what would happen if it doesn't?'

Stunned silence.

The other suits looked on in amazement

'Can we take that chance? then what happens if it is thrown out of court. That won't be good enough. Think about it in the mind of the populace he will have got off by default and will still be guilty. No, we have to make sure that he is found not guilty and that justice has been done.'

'Who is this guy' said Jim, 'an intelligent lawyer'.

'Roderick is right' said the lead lawyer again looking over his half lens glasses, rather embarrassed that he hadn't made the comments. 'The PM has to appear in court and faces his accusers, then we will work our magic. Obviously, it was a set-up; in addition, the judge will be some local public servant, so we can go after him and nail him for his errors.'

Roderick was feeling a little more confident now. 'Let's be careful, that should be a last resort. Perception is everything, we don't want the general public to think that even though they are right that he got off due to legal loopholes. No, we have to create the scenario that he was set up by the police and the city for publicity and then prove it. Then when he gets off, really go to town and get public opinion to feel sorry for him that he was the victim. Yes, even the PM can be a victim."

Crispin, with his bald head gleaming in the lights, speaking to his nearly empty wine glass, 'Don't forget that whatever you say about the police etc. watching and waiting for him to do it the idiot did actually did smoke the joint. Nobody forced it into his mouth.'

The boys were sat there leaning back in their chairs loving every minute of the lawyers' conversation.

'We can paint the circumstances as a set-up, but he is the PM, there should be some semblance of intelligence and maturity and that even though in our eyes he was set up, when offered the joint he could have refused it, or even his 'handlers' should have made sure that he didn't.'

'Don't laugh,' said the senior lawyer laughing, as he looked over his half lenses, 'I have it that they were as stoned as the PM. Let's face it at any public function, even if it was a back yard, with the avaricious media around him any prudent person would not smoke a joint. It's perception, hasn't he got half a brain to realise that? Sorry that's rhetorical.'

'Actually, this guy is growing on me,' Tom smiled, 'they must be looking for divine inspiration. Look more drinks, food as well, they are certainly getting their money's worth out of the Government.'

'More precisely us, the tax payers, with the funds being mis managed by the Government,' said Jim as he carried on like his buddies making notes on paper napkins.

'Anybody know who will be handling the trial? Asked Bert. 'Who chooses the judge? is it done locally or is it the Government?'

'Isn't it done by the local Court administrators,' said Bert. 'No matter what these suits throw at the court about it being a set-up, which obviously it was, we have to make sure that we have a judge who has enough about him to ignore the burden of being harassed by the Government. He has to be strong enough to find the PM guilty for the offence that he did commit. We need an intelligent, eloquent person, who theoretically knows right from wrong, especially in his position. He must set an example that is what the judge has to do'.

The lawyers were drinking and eating away, making notes on how they would detail and expose the set-up.

'A good night's work,' said the senior suit. 'We can spend tomorrow having a look around this place and then head back to put the strategy together.'

'You can come out and handle the defence.' He said looking at the young suit, Roderick.

Youngest by some years, looking like he was not long out of school, Roderick nodded in acceptance.

'You should be in and out in a couple of days, we will make sure that the PM doesn't even need to attend.'

'Arrogant bastards,' said Bert. "I can't wait for the judge, whoever he is, to hear about this.'

Next morning, the boys, the Mayor and Judge Abercrombie, the same Judge Abercrombie of tree huggers and stocks fame, met.

The Mayor and the Judge, who by the way, absolutely detested political interference of any nature, made sure who would be on the bench for the PM's trial.

The boys explained what they knew. Sounds plausible, said Abercrombie. What I don't get though is how you know all this.

'By some sheer flook,' said Tom thinking quickly. 'A panel of the Government's lawyers just happened to not only choose the restaurant where we were having dinner, but we just happened to be on the next table to them.'

'Well!' gasped Abercrombie, 'for being that stupid they deserve everything they get.'

'I hope I am not being too insensitive but,' Tom lying through his teeth, 'we heard that the Government was happy to approve you Judge based upon your age and that you were more likely than others to make the odd mistake, thus allowing them the opportunity to attack the prosecution's case.'

The judge sat there, thinking and appearing unconcerned.

Then he spoke, 'You know what?' his hands and fingers clenched together, 'In a way, the last thing that the PM wants is for this case to be thrown out of court because of a screw up by me.'

He then sat back, folded his arms across his chest. 'This will not, in the minds of the voters prove him innocent. It will just prove to the voters that the Government interfered in due process.

'I am going to enjoy this case,' said Abercrombie his smiling face glowing.

Behind the scenes, the Government lawyers, even though they feel that it was the way to go and didn't hold much hope, were still working on getting the case thrown out. However, not only the populous of Mere Folly but also the majority of the country were vociferous in demanding that the PM face his accusers. The behind the scenes pressure on Mere Folly was tremendous, but the city held out.

Problems arose in Mere Folly, especially to its citizens. Things like pension payments, government payments to businesses, grants were held up. One thing was certain, though, Mere Folleyians now understood the fickleness of the Government. The local newspaper owned by the boys brought it to the attention locally, it was picked up nationally. The newspaper then went to attack the Government with headlines like "small City held to ransom and bullied by the Government".

With word getting around the country, any credibility the Government had, was gone. When the issue was raised by the opposition parties at question time, the PM was called a bully which made him even madder. The media was having a great time, accusing the PM of having no backbone and brain. Because he had no brain; policy, strategy and approach were dictated by others, he was just the front man for a crew of comedians. When a plan failed, he was the fool as in this case.

The boys suggested to the Mayor that he should put pressure on the judiciary, well as much as he could, to get on with the trial. A case was cancelled, the PM's trial was slipped into the diary, the Government protested that three days was not enough notice.

Roderick arrived to begin the PM's defence with Judge Abercrombie sitting. The media arrived en bloc, there were not enough hotels in Mere Folly so those in the City to the south were thrilled, business in Mere Folly was booming. The PM didn't bother to turn up, that was what the Government lawyers were for.

After the first day the Government realised a mistake had been made in giving the job to a schoolboy. Whilst knowledgeable, intelligent and gifted he was no match for the battle-hardened dust eating prosecution team and especially one Judge Abercrombie.

As the judge said, 'In the eyes of the law everybody is equal, therefore the contractor, doctor or barman would be here for the verdict. I expect the defendant to be here.' In fact, the judge insisted he be there.

"I will be in this courtroom in seven days with my decision.

The PM was furious especially at his legal team. He had the sense of impending doom and he wasn't far wrong.

The boys were at the back of the courtroom, no cameras were allowed, it was packed with journalists and the few citizens of Mere Folly who managed to get in.

Amongst the joie de vivre of the occasion, Tom was whispering to his buddies about how concerned he was about the gravity of the situation and that the city would have to be careful going forward. The PM had lots of friends, they were still in power and could hurt Mere Folly.

The Mayor was given the honour of presenting council's recommendation to the Judge, rather strange but something that the Judge had asked for.

The Judge, in his own mind had stood up to similar local and national legal situations previously and was not about to back down. Besides that, it was to be his final act in any form of power.

Bert had invited the Mayor over to his place, eventually he arrived.

'What's the judge's history said Jim, he must have a chink in his armour somewhere.'

'Never heard anything' said the Mayor, he got up and made for the door, 'I don't know why I came. You guys just want to grill me and dig me into a corner you are good at digging muck up on various people, you check him out.'

'Hmmm' said Bert, 'he's still a prick, I need a beer, let's pop to Chat'

'Look who's going in,' said Jim as they walked along the sidewalk on the other side of the street.

Fortunately, Claire was helping a customer at a table, as the Judge waited in line. Bert nipped over to Claire, the Judge was shown to THE table.

The boys walked over to their table at the back of the restaurant. The beer arrived, the ear buds went in, listening began.

The Judge was with an attractive woman who appeared to be a shade younger than him, she was as tall as he was, slim and very well dressed.

'Nice table, they must know you here,' she smiled

'Never been here before, found this coupon,' as he pulled it out the top pocket of his black tailored blazer. 'Look, if you buy an entrée you get one free, that's why I asked you to come.'

'Glad to know that I am not going to break you when you take me out, which isn't that often,' said his lady friend.

'Well there aren't that many times that I come across such valuable coupons.'

'Do you want me to go halves with you on the half price entrée? here's the waitress, are we going to have big or little glasses of water,' she smirked.

The boys were loving it. 'I really like this guy,' laughed Jim and 'she's' not bad, great personality'.

'So, what are you going to do about the PM'.

'Obviously she knows him pretty well,' Jim went on, 'you can tell that they are not married.'

'How do you know that they are not married?' asked Kev.

'It doesn't take a rocket scientist to figure that one out, I'd love to see your wife take that from you and besides that there's a warmth and repartee.'

All went quiet at the boys' table as the Judge started talking again.

'You know, until a few days ago I was adamant that the PM must pay for breaking the law, his father snubbing me and telling me that he would make sure that I wouldn't be a lawyer. We were young and students protesting at the time was the in thing. Why he had to deliberately go out and try to ruin me I don't know, I was one of many, he was a vindictive nasty person. Luckily for me he didn't hang around that much longer to ruin my career, but he tried. It was a tough few years, you moved on, I lost you for the most meaningful years of our lives. Thank goodness I found you again.

'Wow,' said Tom 'there's much more to this, so that's why he's nailing the PM, revenge against his old man. Not only for the grief he caused him, but he's also blaming him for losing his girlfriend.'

'Having thought about it some more, with you in front of me, I am even more convinced that the city of Mere Folly make the PM pay to the full extent of the law. He's like his father and from what I hear from the capital, an immature, vindictive bullying so and so, therefore he will be made to pay dearly.'

The boys gasped. 'I thought for a minute he was going to let the PM down lightly,' Tom whispered. 'No way, he does want revenge, after hearing that who are we to stand in his way, even if we could.'

The boys nodded.

'I think that you should bow out graciously, there is more than one way to skin a cat,' added the lady looking in the Judge's eyes in the way women can when they have a devious idea.

The Judge and for that matter, the boys sat in silence impatiently waiting for her to tell the Judge what she had in mind.

'Think about it; we want to be together and spend our remaining years privately enjoying each other's company. If you go for the PM's jugular, put him in handcuffs and place his head in stocks you really humiliate him, which is what he deserves. The majority of the population in this country will love you. But, and it's a big but, the PM and his cronies will be out to get you, the media will be chasing you, your retirement life will never be your own. I know that you want revenge and you will never rest until you can nail him and I agree with you the bastard needs taking down. Obviously, if you find him guilty, he's a criminal, has it occurred to you he can't be the Prime Minister. I bet the opposition has already recognised that, hopefully he is going to be removed from office. You have started the deed and can watch from a distance, quietly and privately as due process continues and your revenge will be sweet. What do you want to do next?' she asked

She told him to think on it as she got up and left the table and headed for the door.

The final words the boys heard were, 'I will contact the Mayor' as he followed.

The boys were interested. 'Who is the woman?' asked Bert.

'Obviously his new girl-friend,' said Kev.

'Not so new,' interrupted Tom. 'One thing though, there is more to her than meets the eye

'Good news' said the Mayor greeting the boys with his teeth gleaming like a Cheshire cat.

'Yeah,' said Bert, 'it is good news, well done.'

'You mean that you know about the Judge's decision.'

'Of course,' lied Jim,

'Twenty hours of community service isn't enough for that bastard.' Exclaimed the Mayor. 'How do you know that anyway?'

'Come on Mr. Mayor we know most things that go on here.'

'What we do need though is for you to come with us to meet with our local MP, as a member of the opposition, we feel that there is an opportunity for him get a leg up on the political ladder and for you to get the revenge that you have been seeking.'

'I should have known that you four were scheming again.' The Mayor still didn't quite know what was going on.

Thirty minutes later they had the undivided attention of the MP for Mere Folly. Even though he didn't know the boys personally, he, like most people in Mere Folly had heard of them. They had got a message to him that they needed to discuss a matter of National importance which of course what they had in mind was.

'If', Tom launched into his presentation, 'if the Prime Minister is found guilty, and we have it on good authority he will, he will have a criminal record. Most honourable politicians would resign, but he will probably have to be removed from office and then be able to call an immediate Election. We will help you not only to get re-elected but also give you the opportunity to become one of the leaders here as we intend to make Mere Folly a sovereign free state, something like Monaco or Andorra

'You guys are nuts.' said the MP. 'That's a laugh you having a consequence on me being re-elected. I won't have a problem.'

'That's what I said,' interrupted the mayor, 'They helped me.'

'Another arrogant politician,' said Bert. 'Listen, it's up to you. We will make sure that you don't even get nominated to stand in the election. What if we get the Mayor to stand?'

The Mayor was so shocked, he just sat, stupefied.'

'Besides, what will your wife say if we give her the nod about your extra-curricular activities.'

There was silence, a typical Bert tactic. He figured that most politicians had the opportunity to do a bit extra on the side and many jumped at it. Obviously, Mere Folly's MP was no exception.'

'You help us, we will help you,' said Bert to as he thought to himself that the MP must be really involved to give in so easily. 'The other woman must mean a lot to you,' an unusually sensitive Bert added.

A sheepish MP nodded. The boys realised that this just wasn't a scum-bucket politician using his position to play the field.

There was an air of wretchedness as Tom took over. 'We have literally rebuilt this city and pulled it out of the doldrums. We don't trust the political hierarchy, nothing personal, so what we would like to do is divorce, excuse the pun, Mere Folly from the country and set it up as an independent state, much the same as Monaco, Andorra, Luxembourg. We want to set Mere Folly up as a financial and tax haven.'

'What's stopping you? other than the cost.'

'Not so much the cost,' said Tom ruefully, 'but initially the maintenance of the infrastructure and operation of the city.'

'Let me get this right, you want me to go to my party leader and tell him that you want his help to allow Mere Folly to secede from the country but still maintain all the existing facilities and infrastructure. You are nuts! I like it, but it will be impossible.'

'No,' said Kev, 'You are missing the point, it's not what you think, get on the phone right now and tell your boss that we can give him the head of the PM on a platter.'

They had to act fast before the Judge brought down his decision and it became obvious to everyone that the PM could be forced to resign. There would be no chance of negotiation.

'Phone your boss and tell him that we can arrange for the PM to be found guilty and as a criminal he can be asked to resign or removed from office, there will then be an election and he can be the new PM.'

'That's'

'Just do it, now,' ordered Bert, 'Please.' Polite, unusual for Bert, but emphatic.

Ten minutes later the MP handed the phone to Tom, he wants to talk to you.

'How are you sir?' Tom winked at his colleagues. 'Agreed, we shouldn't be discussing this on the telephone.' Where are you?' 'What with your key players.' 'You can arrange transport; we will be there.'

Tom smiled, 'we are off to meet the opposition.'

'Where?' said Jim.

'To the airport, they are going to arrange transport. Sorry Mr Mayor, it's going to look a bit conspicuous if you are spotted with our MP. We will keep you updated.'

'So, when are we going?' asked Jim.

'Now,' said Tom, 'we haven't got any time, we have to nail this now or the chance has gone.'

'I have a tee time,' said Jim

'Piss off,' said Bert, not caring whether Jim was joking or not.

Three hours later, the boys and their MP were sat with the leader of the opposition and his steering committee about two hundred miles south of Mere Folly.

The boys got right down to it. An hour later they had explained their venture, they could tell that the politicians were bemused.

'Let me get this right; you want to set up a sovereign city state, with the country picking up the tab for the cost of providing and maintaining the infrastructure. Residents of Mere Folly will not pay taxes and businesses will be encouraged to operate from Mere Folly due to preferential tax rates.'

'Exactly.' Said Bert.

'You guys are nuts, you expect us to give you all these concessions, what experience do you have?' the boys realized that the opposition was no different, they were all politicians, the politician arrogance was coming out.

By this time Tom had lost it. 'Listen, we are going to do this with or without you. We have put Mere Folly where it is today without your help.'

'What do you mean, you have built Mere Folly, you make me laugh,' went on another conceited politician.

The boys looked at each other and got up in unison. 'Is the transport ready,' asked Jim, 'we've had enough. Enjoy your next four years in opposition, you've had your opportunity and blown it.'

'Hold it guys, said the Mere Folly MP. 'Do you lot even know where Mere Folly is, have you ever been there, do you care.'

'They are not worth the effort; I don't know why you work with a bunch of such self-important cretins.'

The door slammed, 'You should find yourself another party, at least you do have a seat, I bet most of those clowns haven't and aren't likely to get one.' said Bert. 'I guess our shot at independence for Mere Folly is shot.'

'Maybe not,' said the MP. 'I may have a lifeline for you, well for all of us.'

The boys stopped to listen.

'Remember, in the last election the ruling party, whilst getting most of the popular vote came in third. I have been approached on a couple of occasions by them if I would be interested in working with them. I am that close; this episode has really tipped me over the edge.'

There the boys and the MP were, days away from Judge Abercrombie passing sentence on the present PM stuck a couple of hours from Mere Folly.

'Get on the phone to this other party,' jumped in Jim. 'Here is a golden opportunity. Will they be ready if the election happened within weeks?'

'They keep telling me they are, my party isn't, at this stage, my present party wouldn't have a clue what to do.'

'It doesn't take a rocket scientist does it.' Jim was getting excited. 'On the phone, we can meet them anywhere, time is of the essence, but we need quick decisions.'

'Yes, but where are we going to meet them and how are we going to get there,' said the MP not used to acting so quickly and decisively.

In the plane, the one we came in,' said Jim.

'But it's not ours.'

'Who cares, its rented, we'll carry on renting it. The bill will end up with those clowns, if the worse comes to the worse one of the parties will pick it up.'

The boys and the MP were off again, this time on a five-hour flight. The powers that be in the 'other' party were thrilled when they heard that the MP would not only like to cross the floor but in addition was bringing a number of colleagues with a proposal that would have them in power within weeks. The party leader thought it was a joke but the MP guaranteed him that he wouldn't be flying in a private plane to see him and his party leaders if the proposal wasn't for real. The party leader assured his key party members that as time was imperative, they must cancel what they were doing and be available at the appointed time.

The boys and the MP walked into the board room. Tom introduced himself, the boys and the MP and apologised for their dishevelled appearance and addressed the party executive.

'Let me get this right; you want to set up a sovereign city state, with the country picking up the tab for the cost of providing and maintaining the infrastructure. Residents of Mere Folly will not pay taxes and businesses will be encouraged to operate from Mere Folly due to preferential tax rates.'

'We've heard that somewhere before,' said Tom in front of a somewhat apprehensive audience. 'Look, we aren't here for our health, as explained we have worked at putting Mere Folly on the map and feel that we have done quite the job.'

'I would agree with that; you've done a tremendous job. I've been there, seen it, had a drink by the river. Loved it.' The party leader went on, 'in fact my wife fell in love with the place. How can you guarantee that there could be an election very shortly let alone that we could form the government?'

After the compliment, the question took Tom by surprise, but he soldiered on. 'Obviously you are aware of the current court case going on in Mere Folly. With the PM being found guilty and thus having a criminal record, you will have the opportunity as no doubt the opposition will to have him removed from office. Obviously, the PM's party won't win the election. It will be a straight fight between you and the Opposition. With the Honourable Member for Mere Folly here switching sides and a whole lot of information that we can release on Pierre, the Deputy Leader of the opposition, you won't have a problem.

'What do you have on the Deputy Leader?'

'Let's say he had some property interests in Mere Folly and left town in a bit of a hurry. Anyway, before we leave, we would like written confirmation that Mere Folly will become a Sovereign City State.'

'If we do that for Mere Folly then we would be setting a precedent, we would have to do it for others and before you knew where you were, the whole country would be diluted by Sovereign City States.'

'Good point, we did think about this,' said Bert, 'you can make it known that it will be strictly a one off, for what Mere Folly has done for the Country. It will just be like being knighted or getting an honour bestowed on you.'

'That's bullshit.' said a voice from the end of the table.

'Yes, we know, but it will do for the time being,' added Jim. 'Listen this is what we want. We had this drawn up, if you don't sign it, no hard feelings we don't get what we want and of course your chance of forming the next government is nil to zero.'

'Who drew this up?' asked the leader.

'We did, initially on the plane going to meet the opposition, but obviously we didn't need it'

'It looks pretty good,'

'It should, our lawyer fine-tuned it while we were in the other meeting, we fiddled about with it after the meeting and it was ready for us when we landed here.'

'You don't mess around do you?

'We haven't the time, one day we will tell you about the tale of the tape. Are you ready to sign?'

'We will get back to you once our lawyers have reviewed it.'

'Ok,' said Tom. 'We will expect the signed documents at this e mail address by 10 a.m. our time tomorrow morning. Yes, it's still today, just.' We are going back home now.'

'We won't be able to get our lawyers on this until tomorrow.'

'You pay them, don't you?' Said Kev

'Well of course we do.'

'That's what you pay them for, service. Our guys have done all this for us in less than a day. You had better get on the phone now, time is of the essence.'

The boys slept pretty well on the plane. When Bert checked his e mail after a few hours' sleep, he was happy. Later, the four of them sat at the back of Chat, tired but mellow, as they toasted Mere Folly, Sovereign City State.

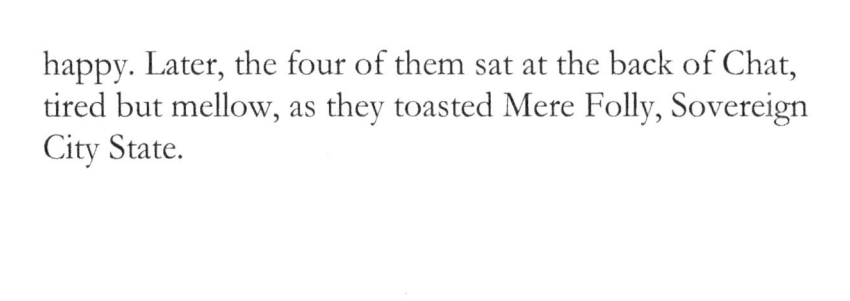

CHAPTER 4.

'Not only were you instrumental in, but you were very involved in the development of the concept of legalising cannabis. Once in force you chose to ignore any nuances to the law that communities adopted. As the driver of this law, the person responsible for the implementation of this law and the leader of the country, you, more than anybody have far greater accountability, hence more is expected of you. This in my mind makes you twice as guilty and you can have no excuse for your actions. I therefore find you guilty and expect that you will be back in my court tomorrow morning at eleven am for sentencing.

There were gasps. It meant that the PM would not be on his plane back to the Nation's Capital that afternoon, but would have to spend another night in a local hotel.

The judge left the courtroom with the PM's lawyers following him. His assistant and the police told them that he would see them at eleven am the next day. Abercrombie was in his element and really enjoying this, no bumptious arrogant prick was going to abuse the law and get away with it.

The PM was in court looking non-too pleased. The Judge had had a phone call from the Lord Chief Justice advising him to be careful as the Nation's eyes were on him. This made the Judge even more irate, but he really didn't give a shit about the powers that be, as it was his chance to get the PM as the end of the month which fell in ten days' time would mark his official retirement.

The clouds were gathering, it was ominous for the PM as he was certain that the punishment he was going to receive was going to be based on revenge and the fact that him and his party were going to be taught a lesson. That afternoon, though, the PM's people were contacted by the MP for Mere Folly and insisted on meeting as he felt he could help the PM but wouldn't elaborate. That evening the PM and a couple of suited individuals met with the MP and were introduced to the boys in the boardroom of the Vineyard condominium.

'Let's call a spade a shovel,' said Tom sitting down next to the PM, who by this time, his arrogance faded, looking rather forlorn was really worried about what would befall him the next day.

Obviously, the boys knew the sentence that would befall the PM and proceeded to tell the PM that they could help him.

One of the suits, immediately jumped in. 'I don't know what you are about to say but it smells highly illegal.'

'Shut up,' said the PM, 'It's alright for you, you aren't about to led to the slaughter.'

Knowing the state of mind of the PM, Tom carried on and then surprised the PM and his entourage when he pulled out the Charter, ready to be signed. The Charter had been very carefully thought out and prepared by the boys' lawyers, The suits gathered round and skimmed through it as Tom said, 'Would twenty hours community service be ok.'

The PM looked at the Charter before him to set up the sovereign state of Mere Folly, his comments regarding the conditions set out in the Charter were none too complimentary. However, after the boys had excused themselves and explained that they would personally throw the first tomatoes at the PM as he sat in the stocks outside Mere Folly City Hall, they were called back and the Charter was duly signed.

Amongst other things, the Charter directed that the citizens of Mere Folly would be exempt from all income taxes, sales taxes, value added taxes for perpetuity, notwithstanding that Mere Folly's infrastructure, schools, hospitals and all other required facilities would be maintained and serviced. In addition, new facilities and services must be added as directed by the sovereign state of Mere Folly as and if required by its board. which again provoked the ire of the PM

'You've set me up.'

'Yes,' said Tom

Whatever the boys thought and had conveyed to the Mayor and especially the judge, the real influence came from the lady in his life. He was on a mission.

'As a warning to others that nobody, whatever status, can circumvent the law and as you have been found guilty of the charge, but as you will now have a criminal record, the court will be lenient and sentences you to twenty hours community service.

Again, there were gasps as the defence lawyer jumped to his feet.

'You can't do this you are dealing with the PM.'

'Oh no,' Tom groaned and rolled his eyes as he turned to look at the boys. Each one of them knew what would come next.

But, much to the surprise of the boys, the Judge was calm, collected and to the point. 'Then he should have known better'. With that he rose and left the court.

In his interview, the senior lawyer, who had been expecting far worse, looked over his half lens glasses and in a forthright stern voice told the world that there would no appeal, and as the PM spends his life servicing the community the Judge's wishes will be obeyed.

The Mayor let the council know in no uncertain terms that although they had the authority to take advantage of the occasion and really punish the PM, it wasn't the wisest way to go.

A number of the councillors told the Mayor that he was being too soft and wanted the weasel nailed to the wall. As the Mayor said, if they weren't careful, they may end up infamous rather than famous. If they were to subject the PM to abuse and nail him to the wall or in this case stocks, rather than a token gesture of punishment they would never get any help from the Government. Put to the vote council voted in favour of the Mayor's proposal.

Within weeks, the actual Charter was in the possession of the boys. Shortly after that the two opposition parties had set the process in place to remove the Prime Minister from office. Before that happened, his party forced him to resign, an election followed. The boys sat on the side-lines watching the ex PM sail into oblivion, but as the boys said over a glass of wine, how could you feel sorry for the pratt as within a year or so he will be given a position somewhere in the diplomatic service at a ridiculous salary or write a book.

The MP for Mere Folly was easily re-elected and his party was heralded into power with a landslide victory.

One of the first things that the new Government did was to keep its promise and work with Mere Folly to ease its way to become a Sovereign City State. With the ex PM's Charter secreted in their lawyer's office, the boys, with that Charter as a secret back up made sure that the benefits of the new Government's charter exceeded those in value.

The people of Mere Folly were thrilled, the local paper produced a special edition explaining what it meant and the benefits to its citizens going forward.

CHAPTER 5.

Well now we live in and control a Sovereign City State, what do we do with it?

There was a moment of silence as the wine arrived.

We can build our own financial and tax haven. People, companies can set themselves up here, we can charge fees up front and let them off with lower tax rates and most importantly free them from the burden of capital gains tax. We have the opportunity to set up a financial empire.

'But Tom, we don't have the office space for all these entities.'

'Bert, all they need is an office with a plaque on the front door basically to say that they are domiciled in Mere Folly and therefore are subject to its tax laws.'

The new Government was backing the boys, they saw it as an 'interesting scenario that could benefit the country'. Its's subliminal message to the boys was to get on with it, as the Government will pick up the pieces as you fail, kick you out and then use the information, data and reasons for failure to develop its own internal financial haven.

The boys held their first board meeting at their table at Chat.

'Do we really need this,' jumped in Jim, 'where we are today just crept up on us. Look at where we are today, we can sit back, relax, watch a well-run, beautiful city and to a certain extent can control our own destiny. I'm quite happy at calling it quits.'

'So, what do you do all day when you are not playing golf?' asked Bert, 'do you read, what keeps your mind ticking over?'

'Exactly,' said Tom. 'As soon as you stop thinking and using your mind you are on your way down the ladder. We need a challenge without the stress. What happens and who cares if we fail at this, we give it to the Government to run, but it helps to keep our minds active and we have had a go.'

Kev had been sat there listening and waiting. 'You know what Jim, I love my golf, but you can only play so much. I'm not going to give it up, this project will allow us to do what we like doing, we are not going to run this thing. How have we been successful? We have got experts to run the various business segments, we watch and manage. Which is what we are going to carry on doing. Nobody is going to stop you playing golf, let's face it you need the practice.'

'I guess you guys are right,' Jim conceded, "But tell me who do we get to run this thing, can we find a person whose ego would allow him to report to us which he would have to and the leading question, will he be able to work with us?'

Another bottle of Amarone arrived, 'You guys have insurance experience, why don't you run it?' Kev was stirring the pot.

'I don't want a full-time job,' responded Jim.

'Is that because you've never had a full-time job?'

'Get serious,' said Jim. 'this is a critical appointment. What do we do advertise, get a head hunter?'

'No, no,' interrupted Tom. 'I've never advertised or used a head hunter, let's face it a resume and an interview doesn't tell you anything. Then there is the reference process, nowadays nobody is going to say anything bad about a person and if you don't want to lose a person you are not going to say anything good about them, it's pathetic. It takes at least six months to a year to get to know a person and by then it costs you time, aggravation and money to get rid of them if you have made a mistake. What does an intelligence or personality test tell you, no, you need to have seen them in action.' That's why we should give this some thought and ask around, any ideas? We don't have to start this project tomorrow so let's start talking to people and spreading the word.'

'What rumours are we going to start?' asked Bert.

'Well let's say we are going to start an insurance company and are looking for a CEO, you never know what might come out of the woodwork, I mean is it an insurance company we want to start? a haven for financial products? The world's our oyster so to speak.'

Tom rounded it out, 'as we say, let's see what turns up, we are in no rush. Why dictate and try and ram a square bolt in a round hole. We can cultivate and prescribe a plan and find nobody who can make it work. No, we are better waiting to see what turns up, what quality there is, what concepts are available and then we can put the gloss on it and develop from there.

Imagine, Mere Folly with its own insurance company providing its citizens with cheap insurance and set up that resident insurance scheme. As we discussed before, we will use a limited amount of capital and use our good friend Elliot or somebody like him and reinsure everything to death. Automobile, home, personal a mandatory program and then all the

City's property without paying tax. There are lots of people living in Mere Folly with insurance expertise, we would be creating employment for the residents. They would love to pop down the road to go to work instead of making the trek that many of them do. We just have to find somebody to run it.

The Deputy Minister had heard about the plan to capitalise a new insurance company, returning Tom's call he asked him to visit him. The boys were laughing as Tom told him that they were busy that particular day.

'Well when can you come and see me,' said an irritated Deputy Minister.

'Why don't you come and see us if it's that important.'

'Listen, if you want to push on with your insurance company then you had better be in my office first thing tomorrow morning' said an even more irritated Deputy Minister.

'Hold on,' interrupted Tom, smiling at his buddies, 'you listen to me. You have no jurisdiction over Mere Folly, we don't need your ok to proceed with any of our plans. Therefore, if you would like to find out more about our plans you will have to make an appointment to visit us.'

Oh dear, guess he didn't like what I had to say, he hung up,'

'Love it,' said Jim, 'everybody is meant to bow down to these bureaucrats, and be afraid of them. The bigger the title the less they know, you are supposed to accept everything that they say or do. Well times they are a changing as Mr. Dylan would say.'

'By the way, who runs the Government compliance department?' asked Bert.

'I presume it's still Paul Bishop,' said Tom
'Good guy?'
'Yes, for a civil servant, he certainly knows his stuff.'

The penny dropped.

'Brilliant Bert,' he can be our first hire, 'not only will we be hiring a quality guy, but it will really piss off the Minister and Deputy Minister.'

'You know what is even better, he just happens to live in Mere Folly, I used to work with him quite a lot and really got to know him? He was so nervous in case it could be construed that he was fraternising with members of the insurance industry. The Deputy Minister was a bit of a bully and Paul was always afraid to socialise in the event he was accused of favouritism. If ever we went to lunch it had to be well outside of the big city downtown core just in case he was spotted associating with the enemy.'

It didn't take Paul long to consider the boys' offer, he even brought two of his department with him.

'Not like you to be late,' Jim sniped as Tom made his way to the table at the back of Chat.

'I was on the phone to Mary Moron's lover, Elliot.'

"Why would he call you?"

'The word is on the street, there are people who want a piece of the action, there are those who just want to know what is going on and of course, being the insurance business there are those that are jealous and want us to fail so that they have something to gossip about over lunch.'

'Why would he call you?' repeated Kev. 'I suppose he wants to resurrect your friendship now you can be useful to him.'

'You are right, he probably asked around his cronies he meets with out here. One thing I have learnt though, friends stick with you through thick and thin.'

There was a pause, but Tom was calm, 'It didn't take him long to hear what we are up to, he happens to be out here next week and would like to meet to see if he can help us'

'Is he bringing the moron to the meeting?' asked Jim. 'I wonder if she even knows he is coming to town?'

'Perhaps we should get the Mayor to ask her.'

Elliot, so he said to Tom, just happened to be coming to town to visit the couple of Companies that he did business with.

The boys were in Chat on the Sunday evening to prepare for the next day's meeting with him. Well, well smiled the boys, as who should wander in and sit at the table but the moron and her friend Elliot.

'Why does she continue to bring him in here or for that matter take him anywhere in Mere Folly?' Asked Bert, 'obviously, everybody knows her here so what's her game.'
In went the ear plugs. They had it down to a fine art now, a synchronized ear plug quartet.

He thought he was captivating the moron with his smooth chatter, to many within the industry it got a bit thin as he always came across as having a slimy personality and was regarded as a bit of a joke.

He congratulated the moron on her City becoming a sovereign city state. 'Was it a difficult thing to pull off?' he asked. He was dumb enough to think that she had been involved in pulling off this coup.

'It was hard work, but I made sure that council got it done.' She lied.

'You should have let me know about it the last time I was with you; with my connections I could have helped.'

Jim gestured sticking his finger down his throat. 'Dumb and dumber they deserve each other, they are trying to excite each other, can't wait to see who outlasts the other or who impresses the other the most.'

Elliot explained to the moron that he had picked up on the industry grape vine that with its new status, the City was aiming to become a financial centre come tax haven. I knew immediately that you would be involved so I arranged a business trip as an excuse to see you. Knowing how important you are we could work together on this.'

'I don't know whether he's bloody good or he is an idiot and actually believes her,' said Bert.

With all that they were involved in in Mere Folly, the moron didn't really know them. To her mind they were just a bunch of hapless seniors, she had no intention of finding out what made them tick or getting to know them. She didn't even cast a glance at them as she made her way and sat at the table.

On the contrary the boys were quite happy to get to know her, even though it was through listening to her from a safe distance.

'So, who are these guys that I am supposed to meet tomorrow? Elliot asked the moron. He was playing the game, pleading ignorance, in the hope of getting some un biased information. 'I know a couple of them worked in the insurance business, but obviously weren't much good if I've never heard of them.' Hearing this the boys winced and smiled. Knowing what they knew, their day would come.

'As I said,' added the moron, 'they are a bunch of seniors who hang around the bars and own a bit of property in Mere Folly. The Mayor seems to like them but that doesn't say much, he hasn't got a clue and let's face it he won't be the Mayor after the next election. All this garbage about a financial centre, they haven't a clue, that's why they are looking for a person to run the insurance company. Tomorrow my darling with your knowledge you will take them to the cleaners. Promise them something that they will buy into and then you and I will take advantage, dispose and destroy them. I will back you so that you become the president of this insurance company, then you and I will take over Mere Folly.

'Love you too,' said Bert smiling.

Next morning, Elliot was sat with the boys, suit, collar and tie, cheesy grin on his face. 'Good of you to see me, I've heard a lot about you and what a lot you have done in the insurance world.' he was getting in to his ingratiating business act in that I don't care what you say, I will tell you what you want to hear mode.

'I will do all I can, I don't care what it takes to get the business.'

All of a sudden, the boys were Elliot's new best friends, but for how long.

The boys had been there, seen it, done it and after listening to the previous night's performance all they wanted to do was vomit.

'So, what can I do for you? Tom and I go back a long way. It will be good working with you again?'

Tom bit his lip. What price loyalty, since he retired, and was of no use to him, or so Elliot thought, Elliot had ignored him. Tom desperately wanted to tell the arrogant arsehole that there was nothing that he could do for them that another ten companies out there could do better. The boys looked at each, they knew only too well to let him get on with it and they would pick up the pieces later.

'Tell us about you and your company and where your expertise lies,' said Bert.

'No problem,' said Elliot and he set off on a spiel that he had probably used many times.

The boys didn't say a word.

'Any questions?' Elliot asked.

That was the cue for Tom. 'Not really, what you do is quite complex and that's why we need somebody like you to help and guide us. Can you draft a proposal as to how you see this working and what we need to do going forward?'

'A kind of business plan?'

'Yes Elliot, with strategy and financial projections would be perfect,' went on Kev.

'Can I buy you gentlemen lunch? we can get to know each other a little better.'

'Oh no,' said Jim would love to but we have another piece of business we have to attend to.'

That was a bit of shock, in Elliot's world, nobody ever refused a free lunch.'

Off he went promising a proposal and business plan that would enable Mere Folly to become a major insurance centre.

Bert was amused, 'Thank goodness we listened in to him and the moron, it substantiated what we already know, the guy is an arrogant prick and the two of them deserve each other. What's the mayor going to say when we tell him that the two of them are going to take over Mere Folly and he is toast.'

'Should we tell him?' Jim asked the proverbial rhetorical question, clearly knowing the answer as did the others.

'Mark my words,' said Kev, 'the day will come when we will be delighted to use that piece of information and I state hear and now that I would like that opportunity.'

'I tell you one thing though,' said Jim, 'it was a great way to get the first draft of a business plan.'

As Elliot had some time to kill at lunch time, he phoned the moron. They met in his hotel room and as they collected themselves after a session of extra-curricular activity, they lay under the bed clothes discussing Elliot's meeting.

'You were right, they are a bunch of simpletons, haven't got a clue.'

'Where did you leave it,' the moron asked as she lay on her back with her hands behind her head.

'I thought we had finished, weren't you satisfied' he said, 'we can always make time to finish it.'

'No, you sex maniac, what's the next move?'

'Anything you want.' He said. 'Ok, ok, only joking. No, I will get the business plan to them, offer to put everything together.'

The moron was thinking aloud. 'There has to be a city committee to run the thing, I will get myself chosen as chairman and bring you in as CEO or President and then we can literally take over.'

She got dressed, 'meet you at 7 at Chat to fine tune the plan.'

'Do we have to go to that place again?'

'I am hoping the Mayor will come in and see us together or hear from somebody that we were together.'

'What's it matter as to whether we are together or not?'

'I want him to know that I know you and am responsible for bringing you in on the project,' she said lying through her teeth, knowing that if he saw her the Mayor would be as jealous as hell.

Tom sent a text to Bert, Kev and Jim, he had just received one from Claire.

'Guess who's made a reservation for the table.'

They were sat there sipping their beer as the moron arrived and shortly after, Elliot appeared.

'Hmmm, quite the lunch break,' said Elliot as he sat down across the table from the moron

'Yes, it made me rather hungry,' she said.

'I was hungry before I got there,' he went on

'So pleased I satisfied that hunger.'

The boys looked at each other. 'Pathetic,' said Jim, 'like two school kids, we should have invited the mayor I am sure that he would have enjoyed himself listening to this. Perhaps we should text him to come over.'

'You must be joking,' said Tom 'I am sure he'd be happy knowing that we've bugged the table and in addition I couldn't put up with a grown man crying.' I wish I could ask the romantic duo a bunch of questions

'What do you think of my idea then?'

'Love it,' as she stroked his hand and looked into his eyes. 'With you running the city financial centre and the insurance company and me as chairman of the committee to oversee the setting up and operation of the new sovereign city state.

'Are you sure that you can get yourself elected to chairman?'

Leave that to me, I have the Mayor in my pocket, he's pitiful, he will do anything I tell him to and he rules the council with an iron fist'. 'Let's drink to us my darling.'

The boys were amazed.

'Wow she's really up on herself and talk about pathetic, she's infatuated by the guy, he's going to tread all over her, I can't believe it, I nearly feel sorry for her.' said Kev.

'Where does she think that the resources and capital are coming from,' said Bert. 'does she honestly think that all she has to do is sit on council and let her bimbo put a financial sphere together, she is stupid!'

'Thank goodness for that,' chuckled Tom.

Elliot was on his plane home bright and early the next morning, not that he got much sleep with the moron taking advantage of her husband's business trip. She was a bit disappointed having not been able to introduce the Mayor to Elliot she had tried hard enough to be at places the Mayor frequented so that she could make him jealous. She left Elliot to get ready for his flight and set off back to Mere Folly. It didn't enter his head that what he was about to get involved in something that was out of his league but more to the point, illegal as over a few nights in his hotel room she explained her plan

Driving back to Mere Folly the phone went, sure enough it was the Mayor. 'Where have you been?' she snarled at him, not that she was missing him, she was still annoyed that he hadn't caught her with the new man in her life. She was having a good time, having it off with Elliot, while her husband was away and the Mayor thinking that she was entertaining a business colleague. Well she was but to a greater extent than the Mayor realised.

I was looking for you to introduce you to Elliot.'

'I was busy.'

'Busy with her?' said a slightly jealous moron.

'What do you expect me to do?'

'I expect you to get rid of her and spend some time with me,' she was really milking it. 'I was working, entertaining that guy from the insurance company. Trying to get him to help me get our project on the road'.

'What do you know about insurance?'

Nothing, but I don't need to know a lot, as long as I can use the right people, I'll put it together.'

The moron's choice of words was very carefully chosen, she really did mean use in its true literary sense.

Elliot gave the boys' 'specs' to his company's experts and then set off south with some insurance company executives for five days of golf, drinking and of course picking up women. They had been doing this for about five years, the same women that they met on their first trip still kept in touch and still spent the long weekend with Elliot and his colleagues. Of course, there were numerous meetings with the women throughout the year, with the best part being that the cost was met by the executives' expense accounts.

The presentation was put together, Elliot was going through it at his home, the night before he was due to fly out again to Mere Folly. The woman he was living with for the time being was an engineer and had heard about Mere Folly and its some of its ingenious design features.

'I should come with you.'

Elliot tried to keep calm. 'I'll only be there for a few days and pretty well tied up most of the time.' His mind was racing, that's the last thing he wanted, Christine and Mary to meet.

'Well take some time off and show me around,'

'I am sure that I will be out there in the summer, much better time of the year to show you around.'

It's almost as if you don't want me to come out with you. Just the same as when you go down south or on your other trips.'

'But that's strictly business.'

'Of course, it is, you are talking to me remember, not one of your slugs, I have met those drunks you play golf with and I wouldn't trust them as far as I could throw them.'

Next morning the moron was on the phone to Elliot asking him if he had the presentation for her.

'I've got the presentation,' he told the moron, 'but what are you going to do with it.'

'I'm going to review it and ask you to present it to the council.'

'Why are we presenting it to the council those guys I met asked me to prepare the presentation for them.'

'I think you are missing the point, the council runs Mere Folly, not those four degenerates.

'Oh, ok.' said a baffled Elliot, 'let me know when and where.'

When the Mayor found out what she was doing he was apoplectic. 'Are you nuts? this is nothing to do with the council this is an independent business matter outside of the city's scope. The city isn't a business.

'Listen,' she said, 'the city of Mere Folly is going to build this financial entity, own and operate it.'

'Ok so who is going to run it?'

'I am,' she said.

'But you can't even manage your own cheque book let alone run a financial operation.'

'I am going to run it in conjunction with a person I know.'

'You are nuts,' said the Mayor storming out of her office.

Half an hour later the Mayor was in the boardroom of the boys' condo building explaining his conversation with the moron. Instead of a scene of anger which he mayor expected, the boys burst out laughing.

'So, she is going to build a communist state, wherein all property is publicly owned and she is going to be the dictator,' said Tom.

'What do you mean?'

'Well who is going to want to do business with a communist City State.'

'Oh, I see,' said the Mayor. He didn't really but it was all optics as far as he was concerned

'What are you going to do then?' said the Mayor

'Probably nothing,' said Bert as the others smiled in agreement.

'You mean that you are going to give up on your idea and let her have it.'

'For the time being, yes,' said Bert.

The Mayor didn't get it and looked non-plussed.

'Listen,' said Bert, 'when the presentation is over and friend Elliot asks for questions, this is what we want you to do.

Elliot arrived at the City Hall for the meeting. The Moron introduced him and Elliot read through the power point. A knowledgeable person could tell that

Elliot didn't prepare the power point or even understand it for that matter, but of course nobody in the council chamber understood it either.

'Thank you, ladies and gentlemen,' said Elliot 'can I answer any questions?'

There was silence; how can you ask questions when you don't understand what has been said?

'I have one,' said the Mayor. Of course, there is always the exception, which happens of course if you have been told what question to ask, whether or not you understand the question that you are asking.

'Yes,' Mr. Mayor, said a somewhat surprised moron.

What money will be required to capitalise the insurance company?'

This was a question that Elliot could answer, his team had based the presentation on a specific requirement and briefed Elliot on it.

Elliot felt confident in that he didn't have to bullshit as he actually knew the answer to this one. 'Mr Mayor, the presentation was based upon a capital requirement of one hundred million initially.'

'Dollars?' said the moron.

Again, there was stunned silence.

The Mayor now realised why the boys didn't appear to be too bothered about the moron and her friend taking control, the potency of their question put the cat among the pigeons.

The moron sat there absolutely shell shocked, she looked daggers at Elliot, their relationship soured instantaneously. He left the chamber not quite understanding what was happening.

The Mayor looked at the moron. 'How are you going to raise that much money? Surely you didn't think that you just stuck a nameplate on a wall and take in insurance premiums. I am sure the people of Mere Folly will enjoy coughing that kind of money up.'

The remainder of the councillors broke it into laughter.

'She's as mad as a box of frogs,' said one of the councilors, what a waste of time that was.

CHAPTER 6.

Elliot had forwarded his company's presentation to the boys and was eager to meet with them to discuss. He only had two clients in that area, a third would be perfect in order that he could justify his frequent trips. The money spent on visiting and entertaining his two clients was quite excessive, but that was the way Elliot conducted business. Wine dine and party, he had found a weak link and it was easy for him to bullshit his way through as the guy responsible for the reinsurance, nicknamed ' the weasel' by his staff knew nothing about insurance. How the weasel got where he was nobody knew. Did he have dirty photographs or insider knowledge of the President of the Company? He was one of those people that you took an instant dislike to with the probable exception being his wife, the weasel so much wanted to be a top-level executive. He was jealous of their power, business lunches, corner offices.

He had the responsibility for reinsurance thrust upon him. Although he hadn't a clue as to what he was doing or how it all worked he had a couple of members of staff who handled it. One day Elliot popped in to introduce himself, took the weasel out to lunch and suggested he helped him when the renewal came up. By the time the weasel staggered in through the back door at around 4 pm, he was feeling no pain. He managed to make his way to his office, closed his door, awaking at around 7 pm. He phoned his wife to say that he had had a project dropped on him but was on his way home. Out of literally nowhere, the weasel was copying Elliot buying suits, shirts that needed cufflinks and fancy ties. He was so infatuated with looking the part that on dress down day for charity, he still rolled up in his suit and tie. There was one thing wrong with his office, it was in the centre of the floor plate. Within weeks, he had a corner office built and his old office which was half the size was demolished.

Elliot was out to visit the weasel every couple of weeks, that was when they weren't golfing down south or at a hockey game down south. Elliot sucked up to him, he couldn't stand the guy but it was like shelling peas, the account was his. The paid for trips to the reinsurer's head office, more golf games, fishing trips the weasel was loving it and he still hadn't got a clue as to how reinsurance worked. Then the piece de la resistance, the paid for trip to London, limousine rides, posh lunches, swanky hotels, dinner at the Savoy and the theatre. There were one or two legitimate meetings, a bit of a struggle for Elliot's colleagues as they struggled to cover up the weasel's inadequacies.

Arriving back in the office, most people would have covered over the glitz and the glamour, painting instead a hard-working business trip. Not the weasel he was straight into it. The staff choked. Couldn't believe the money that was spent especially the two who did all the work while he partied. One guy in particular had had enough, an anonymous message found its way to the President's desk and to a couple of the board members.

If the message had of just gone to the President, it would have been swept under the carpet. How could he chastise the weasel when they went out drinking together most lunch times, went on dubious business trips together, which were glorified parties,

The board members called for an instant audit and interviewed the staff. The President ignored the weasel and lunches together over the following week were no more.

It was a big account to Elliot, an association that owned an insurance company. Poorly run but with all its members it had a ready stream of business.

Elliot arrived at the office reception, ready to take the weasel to lunch.

'He's not here' said the receptionist.

'I have an appointment is he due back shortly?'

Just then, a staff member wandered through and just couldn't help himself. Delightedly he smiled at Elliot. 'He was fired this morning and was walked out the door.'

Why? Said a dazed Elliot.

'If anybody should know, you should,' and walked off.

Now most people would be surprised then a little bit shocked and upset, not Elliot. So, who's taking over? he asked the receptionist. Of course, she looked at her computer screen and carried on typing.

The weasel had bitten the dust, he couldn't help Elliot anymore and in Elliot's eyes was immediately persona non grata. Elliot panicked, he needed to find the weasel's successor quickly so that he could ingratiate himself to him or her and not lose the account.

It was a blue-sky spring day, for the first time that year the boys were able to enjoy a glass of wine outside Chat on the Canal. They were taking a look at Elliot's presentation.

Makes sense said Bert but I would never do business with that guy, we asked him to prepare the presentation yet behind our backs he was working with the moron. We know that there aim is to shaft us, even though it was our concept and we were his client.

Just then Tom's phone rang.

'Amazing, talk of the devil, that was our good friend Elliot.'

We gathered that,' said Jim. 'I got the message he wants to meet, do we have to, why didn't you tell him to piss off as we don't like him.'

'I agree with Tom that we should meet him, let's not bring ourselves down to his level. I thought that we should tell him that we don't want to work with him to his face,' said Bert.

'Anyway,' said Tom, 'he is on his way here. He just happened to be here seeing some clients.'

'Sure he was,' smirked Jim.

'I don't know if you gathered it from our conversation but he was really adamant that we meet at his hotel in case he ran into the moron. I told him that we were too busy to go to his hotel, but not to worry as the Mayor and the moron were out of town at a conference so he could relax."

'How do you know that? asked Kev.

'I don't.'

About an hour later, Elliot rolled up. 'Good to see you again gentlemen,'

'Yes,' said Jim.

After ordering drinks, Elliot asked for menus.

'I don't know about you guys but I'm starving.'

'I tell you what,' said Bert getting up,' why don't we just order some food, family style, let me go inside and fix it up.'

'Good idea,' said Elliot, my treat.

As if there was an option thought Bert under his breath. He went to his chef, tell you what Andrew there's five of us, keep the food coming, top of the line and by the way he's paying, double the bill.' Andrew smiled and set about preparing the family style food.'

'Wow this is great and what a great spot,' said Elliot. 'By the way do you guys like fishing,'

'Take it or leave it,' said Tom.

'No, you'll love it, we have a fishing trip up north in July. All inclusive, the flight up there, great lodge, great food fantastic fishing and we even pay for the fish you catch to be frozen and transported to your house.'

Just then the first plates of food arrived.

'This is great you guys, we had better have some more wine.'

They listened and yawned as Elliot rambled on about his golf, women, trips, drunken orgies. More food arrived. Then he turned back to the fishing trip and how the card games ran into the morning and the booze kept flowing.

'And this is all on your company Elliot.'

'You bet.'

'What happens if our concept doesn't succeed and we don't produce much business for you,' said Tom.

'No problem,' laughed Elliot, we'll have had a good time trying.'

Although Elliot was still gorging himself, they called it a day on the food,'

Elliot caught the eye of the waiter, 'You can just bring the bill,'

The boys tried to look innocently on as the bill arrived and Elliot looked at it. Even though he tried hard, there was a certain amount of discomfort in his face.

'Here's to expense accounts,' said Jim holding up his glass.

Elliot was placing the receipt in his wallet, 'when do you want me to start the ball rolling.'

'Actually, we don't,' said Tom.

There was a startled look on Elliot's face.

No, went on Tom, 'we are looking for loyalty, have you ever noticed those that use others? It doesn't matter how you help them, when you are of no use to them, they abandon you and you become surplus to requirements. That's what we have learned about you and why we don't want to do business with you'

The boys got up and walked off, leaving Elliot sat at the table by the canal.

'To really make his day, all he needs now is for the moron to walk by,' said Kev.

After that lunch the boys definitely needed exercise. For the sake of their health they decided to go for a stroll along the canal on their way to Chat.

'We need to sit down and figure out where are going next'. said Kev. 'Look we have a golden opportunity here with Mere Folly becoming a sovereign city state. We can control the council through the Mayor, I don't think that he is going to get any hassle from the moron for the time being.'

'Let's get this financial outpost built and operating said Tom, we now have a review and some actuarial reports as a base.'

They knew that they couldn't use the stuff that Elliot's company had put together but they had a yardstick to use when talking to some of the other players out there when equating their submissions.

'Why don't we use Elliot's stuff?' asked Jim

'Firstly, it's not his, he wouldn't have a clue how to put anything like that together, and secondly, he's in this for one thing, himself, once we out-serve our use to him he would turf us anyway, exactly as Tom said he did to him in the past. Tom's anecdote sums that prick up, we are all believers in fate and him arriving on our doorstep wasn't a flook it was fate. I am sure that he honestly couldn't believe his luck when he saw Tom again and that he was a shoe in to pick up more business. He would also have the added bonus of a taking advantage of another woman on the side, Mere Folly would be one of his hideaways, to where he could flit off every now and again and have some all-expense paid fun on the backs of others.'

Bert went on to explain the story and the profundity behind Tom's message to Elliot, he loved repeating that piece of prose as it sums up his experience of how Tom had helped Elliot get the only three accounts he ever had and then when Tom needed help, as the words went, "we are looking for loyalty, have you ever noticed those that use others? It doesn't matter how you help them, when you are of no use to them, they abandon you and you become surplus to requirements. That's what we have learned about you and why we don't want to do business with you."

'Now I understand,' said Jim, 'that Elliot is really sick!'

'Exactly,' said Tom, 'when you get to your sell by date people use you. You mentor, give people your expertise they use you after that, just like Elliot does and had done in the past. 'What price loyalty.'

Now that we have proved our point, let's forget about the past, the future offers us a golden opportunity, let's get on with it.'

Next morning, the boys were in the big city, it was overwhelming once again for their lawyers and accountants, they just couldn't believe what the boys were now up to. How could four seniors be half way to developing a tax-free haven, already negotiated with the government of the land and critically, it appeared to be legitimate.

The lawyers took the quasi-business plan which although rather weak, Bert explained would give them a flavour of the project.

'We are not going to use it, I don't think that the people that created it fully understood the venture and would probably sue us, however we will have more intense and detailed plans for you shortly.'

Over the next few months, people came and went trying to sell themselves and their company rather than understand what the boys envisioned and help them put the concept into reality.

'You know,' said Kev,' it's become abundantly clear, that you guys know more about what is involved than these quasi experts. Why don't you take it over and put it together?'

'Kev,' said Tom, 'I know I am speaking for Bert as well. That's exactly what we don't want, we've retired and yet we've got lots on our plate.'

Then Jim got excited and suggested that they hired a company to oversee it. Use one of the big brokerage firms, let them handle it and we can manage them, just the same as we do with the rest of our stuff. Knowing something about this business is a good thing gives you a leg up, we have a newspaper but we don't run that do we? We have a couple of good managers. Go back to one of our first discussions – no micro managing, remember?'

When the hodge podge of data, actuarial reviews and plans had been assembled and analyzed, the boys made up a short list of people that they referred to them to interview. The first couple of interviewees with qualifications coming out of their backsides couldn't grasp what the boys were presenting to them. They had absolutely no idea what the boys were trying to do. When asked what they understood a sovereign city state was and what its purpose was, both of them looked puzzled. As far as the boys were concerned, that meant the end of the interview.

'I guess that there was no paragraph on sovereign city states and the insurance and tax benefits in the insurance handbook that these guys probably memorized but didn't understand,' said Bert. That's why the insurance industry is literally a mess, if you have memorized the courses and passed the exams rather than understanding the content and concept and being able to apply it in the real world then you can get a job. Insurance companies are only interested in people that have passed exams. Not whether they can apply what they have memorized and of course they can't teach common sense of street smarts. What annoyed me was that the first two candidates didn't appear to have done any research. All that first guy could talk about was how many letters he had after his name.'

From what they assumed would be a long day of interviews, was all over by lunch time. The boys hadn't the patience to prolong the agony, it didn't take long to figure out that the interviewees were a complete and utter waste of time.

This is stupid said Tom; we are going back to what we said we would never do. We are doing things the conventional way. We are assuming that people who do a great interview, have lots of courses and because they can talk the talk will actually be able to do the job. Then you realize that they can't work in the real world, they become a liability and you end up spending an inordinate amount of time trying to get rid of them.

They were concerned, no surprised, in that they hadn't managed to come across anybody to run the financial company side of things.

'Sure.' Said Tom 'there are all those people with the background who have worked in the environment and have lots of qualifications, but they have no flair and nobody asked the question of what we are doing and what we are trying to achieve. They just want to come in do a job and number crunch what is actually there and go home when the bell rings at the end of the day. They have no idea on how to create

That's what is wrong with governments and councils, they are filled with silly servants who basically just want to work from 9 until 5 take advantage of the benefits and wander off into the sunset with their index linked pensions. What happens in between is immaterial, they are not encouraged to be inventive or creative

The council is even worse, a bunch of part timers, each one, pretty nigh useless it can't run a small city, look what a mess they were making of Mere Folly until we came on the scene so how they are going to take it to the next level and what we envision goodness knows.

The boys were sat in Chat stumped as to where and what to do.

What's the matter with you four' said Giselle as she delivered their beer. You look as if you have the weight of the world on your shoulders.'

'We have,' said Jim. 'It's those idiots on what we call our council.'

'You are right,' she said, 'I don't know why we need a council for all the use it is.' and wandered off.

'She's a genius.' Said Tom.

The others stared at him over their beer.

'She's right, why do we need a council.'

'We have to have a council, or some ruling body,' said Bert, 'In case you hadn't noticed, this is a democracy.'

'Maybe, but is the sovereign state of Mere Folly a democracy.'

"I don't know said Kev. What's that piece of paper the Government gave us say?'

'Never really read it,' said Jim

'Exactly,' said Tom

Two days later they were visiting the lawyers

'Obviously, you guys don't know this, but you have been given the authority to run Mere Folly.'

'What do you mean?'

'The four of you have been named as the ruling council.'

'We just assumed,'

'Quite wrongly,' interrupted the lawyer.

Back in Chat, the boys were discussing what they should do next. Tom came to the conclusion that they should disband the council.

'Great,' said Bert, 'So who is going to run the place?'

'Well I guess our name is on the Charter, We will.'

'Oh no,' exclaimed Jim, 'we are already doing more than we ever expected or intended to do.'

'Who has some experience, will report to us and of course be our puppet?

The boys toasted the new executive administrator of the sovereign city.

'He's obviously well known here, if it went to an election he would win by acclamation, there won't be a problem.' said Tom. 'It will be an easy transition; a logical appointment and we can stay in the weeds.'

If the boys were concerned about the Mayor taking the new appointment, they need not have worried. It went straight to his ego.

The mayor wanted his installation as the executive administrator of the sovereign state of Mere Folly to be a glamour event followed by a banquet and all the trimmings.

That was the last thing the boys wanted therefore the glamour event never happened.

The moron was in her hairdressers telling her about the special event that evening. 'I am going to be presented with an award for my work in having the cross walks painted and the artwork dotted around the City.'

'So, it was you,' luckily the hairdresser stopped herself. 'Who is awarding you that' said Louise, realising that councillor moron's money was as good as anybody else's.

'The Art's Council of Mere Folly,'

'Isn't that nice, but aren't you the chair person,' again taking her foot out of her mouth, 'congratulations.'

That evening she was presented with the award for the significant art contribution of the year. In her acceptance speech the moron went on to explain that even though the cost of the artwork was quite substantial, the citizens of Mere Folly would not be paying for it. The number of speed cameras in Mere Folly have been increased trifold to foot the bill. Invitees at the dinner were amazed that councillor Moron would actually admit to that, but that didn't matter as she smiled at their bewildered looks.

In his closing remarks, councillor Branch, not a great fan of councillor Moron seized upon the opportunity of a lifetime.

'I am sure that the citizens of Mere Folly thank councillor Moron for her contribution to art in the City. It's rather a shame, that for six months of the year we won't be able to see it as it will be covered in snow and mud. Then once the snow removal people with their graders, the sodium chloride and rain etcetera have finished, there will be nothing left to look at. The attractiveness of this art is that, and I know this is going to difficult, but as long as we manage to dodge the speed traps, we won't have to pay for it. However, if the vast proportion of you citizens do manage to escape a fine, then you will be paying for the non-existent artwork by way of your taxes.'

Councillor Moron was apoplectic with Councillor Branch's speech and left in fury clutching her award. The remainder of the people in the room just laughed. The laughter soon died as they started to discuss the stupidity and implications.

If councillor Moron thought that the previous evening was bad, then the next day was even worse. Along with the other members of council she was invited to a special meeting. The EA's first job was to dissolve the council, telling them that it wasn't required as the Charter dictated that the sovereign state was going to be operated by a board. Further, he explained that the new sovereign state was going to be run as a business with a board made up of four people with business acumen.

Upon hearing that she was about to lose her job and more importantly to her, her title, she was beside herself.

The citizens of Mere Folly were bewildered at the chain of events but when advised that property taxes would be a thing of the past, were on board. There were a few general shit disturbers as Bert called them, asking the EA things like where the money was coming from to pay for the costs of running and maintaining the city.

Then the newspaper, whose mandate was to ensure that the populace be kept very well informed of changes and benefits explained how they would not be expected to pay any property taxes, sales tax, federal taxes or income taxes. There would be a general residential insurance plan which would keep premiums at a far lower level than they had ever been used to.

Mostly positive letters to the editor poured in. The new EA wrote a letter in response to the newspaper explaining that this was negotiated with the Government as part of the Charter when the sovereign state was set up. The EA became an instant hero, the members in parliament and citizen's in the rest of the country were making the new PM's life pretty intolerable as they wanted to be treated the same. As the boys and the EA specified over a beer in Chat, 'they really didn't care.'

Just like the chicken and egg situation, which came first the board or the executive administrator? Did the board choose the EA or did the EA select the board? Nobody appeared to question the appointments; the citizens of Mere Folly were thrilled with the benefits that were being presented to them and the euphoria had created a sense of laxness and lasse fair attitude that enabled the mayor to just walk into the new position. Of course, the new position of EA was created and defined by the board named in the Charter, but that four-person board hadn't been made public!

The logical question, asked by a member of council, was whether he could apply for membership of the board.

'Of course, you can,' advised the EA, 'I hope other council members will e mail with their applications.'

Three weeks later, the first board meeting took place. It was called to order by the EA. It wasn't long, actually seconds, before the boys took over. from him

Kev brought up the meeting that they had with the deputy minister. 'Remember, he asked where the business was going to come from. We told him that the base would be the mandatory residents' insurance scheme. One of the bureaucrats told us that we couldn't do that. It's good to know that we are the Government and that we can do that now. We are going to operate this sovereign state for the benefit of its citizens and what we are proposing, no, going to do will benefit its citizens. I am not in the insurance business so I have no axe to grind, but like a lot of people I know we are all eternally frustrated by lack of service from the insurance world.'

Since the initial idea was floated and our discussions with the deputy minister, a lot of water has flowed under the bridge. No longer do we have to bow down to regulators, so let's start with the business plan we gave to the deputy minister, fine tune it with the data from the reinsurers and get this thing moving, after all if you three worked in the business it can't be that difficult to understand.'

The beauty of working without bureaucrats is that projects are finished a lot better and much faster. Within a couple of months, the capital required was in place, people in the industry residing in Mere Folly were jumping at the chance to work locally although that was no solace as they still have to find somebody to run the machine.

It suddenly dawned on Tom. 'Where do we start?'

A personal insurance program for citizens of Mere Folly

Then why not look at other similar programs and who runs them

Jim was about to take a sip of his wine, 'Talking about programs, remember Greg the geek, doesn't he work for that crown corporation, you know the sole provider of automobile over there that would be a perfect model for us. It doesn't provide service, ingenuity or profitability but it actually exists and runs, we can take their model fine tune it into one that actually works, provides service and makes money.

'Yes, but he doesn't run the place, said Tom.
'No but he knows it inside out,' said Jim

'I remember Greg,' said Tom, 'lots of ideas, but he couldn't and perhaps doesn't want to manage or run anything. The last thing he wants to do is to work hard and take responsibility'.

He doesn't need to run it we can do that we need somebody to be there and administer the thing. We could surround him with quality and data and report to us,

Greg was the perfect foil for the boys in operating the insurer. His knowledge of government run auto was a bonus. In addition, he had an understanding of the real world and an entrepreneurial spirit unusual in government employees. In fact, his ingenuity was dying to come out. Tom who had known Greg for about twenty years picked up the phone and within three days was sat with him outside Chat on the canal.

Tom and Bert took on a whistle stop tour of Mere Folly explaining what they had done over the years and how it all came together. He was rather subdued, what he couldn't understand was how four seniors raised the capital and had the acumen to put together an insurance company in such a short time. They went on to explain how Mere Folly was now a sovereign city state and what that meant. All of a sudden Greg's eyes lit up as he recognised there was an opportunity and this was something he would like to get involved in. This was to some degree what he had dreamed about and written reports on for years. With the basic personal insurance program creating the platform, income and credibility, he could see the synergies developing to build and generate lots of benefits.

Undeniably they ended up at their table in Chat, 'who will be doing the reinsurance, accounting, legal's etc,' piped in Greg, now he was as fired up as could be.

'If you sign this non-disclosure form, we can leave this business plan with you.'

Greg thumbed through the plan. 'I see you have this company down as a potential partner, you are not going to deal with that prick Elliot, are you?'

Don't panic,' said Bert, 'I had forgotten you knew him.'

'Knew him,' The boys were seeing a side of Greg that they didn't know existed. All of a sudden, he was angry and emotional. 'I spent the best part of a year helping him and then as soon as he got what he wanted, he ignored me.'

Tom interrupted, 'When something like this happens, you think that you are the only one that gets treated badly or shafted, but we have all been in the same boat.'

'One day, years later,' carried on Greg, 'out of the blue he phoned me saying he would be in my neck of the woods could we get together. I knew exactly what he wanted. To get him in the door and lay our account on a plate for him.'

'So how did your meeting and the free meal go?' Asked Tom.

'There wasn't a meeting or a meal, I just put the phone down.'

'That's why I like that guy,' said Jim after Greg had left. 'No messing about, although he's rather anal he'll fit in well.'

Sat in Chat, Claire was placing a bottle of Chat's house plonk red and four glasses on the table.

Kev was still deep in thought, 'There's our good friend the EA over there,' Claire gave him the evil eye.

'So, what does he tip?'

'He's one of the tight ones, about ten per cent but always rounds it down to an even number'.

'Tight sod,' snarled Bert.

'No, no,' interrupted Kev, 'that's about right, or is it? What's a tip? What's it for?

'Service,' jumped in Jim.

'How come you have to pay for service? I mean you come to a restaurant, what do you expect? Somebody just comes and slaps the food on your table, surely service is included in the meal price? Perhaps restaurants are looking at it differently. Obviously, they list the prices of the food and the drinks, if they want the customer to pay for all the extras, like service and ambiance they should include it on the menu.

'Well, some restaurants automatically include a service charge.' said Bert, 'but you have no choice if the service is lousy.'

'Exactly,' preached Tom. ' The food and drink prices are on the menu, the ambiance adds to the experience and so does the service, without them your dinner is spoiled. So why do you have to pay for service, isn't that what the waiter is paid for, to provide it. You don't tip the chef or the sous chef as part of the cost of your piece of beef is to pay the guy for cooking it.'

'What you are saying then is that the staff aren't paid enough and need subsidising. Therefore, you end up paying extra at the end to subsidize their wages.'

'Well as long as you don't have to tip for lousy food and or service. If the food is awful then you send it back, complain and refuse to pay.'

'Good luck,' said Jim, 'the majority of the people in here will tip no matter what the food or service is like. It's become a habit, a culture, a bloody costly one.'

'What I don't like.' Added Kev 'is those stupid credit card machines that are fixed by the restaurant where the tip starts at eighteen or even twenty per cent. Another thing why is the tip based on price.' Kev was really getting emotional with his rant. 'Think about it, I order a $50 bottle of wine and you order a $100 bottle of wine and we both pay a twenty per cent tip. Therefore, I pay $10 and you pay $20 for exactly the same service, it's stupid. So why not say, a fixed service fee. of x amount of dollars will be added.'

'Great.' Said Tom but what about the party that stays for an extra hour drinking coffee.'

'It is balanced by the party that only stays half an hour or an hour'

The discussion rambled on long into the evening…..

CHAPTER 7.

Jim look flustered as he wandered down to the boys at their table.
'Look at him, somebody must have trodden in his cornflakes, he's completely ignoring the women.
'What's up with you, the clubs not working today?' asked Kev.
'No,' said a flustered Jim, 'I had to come back through town and I find another monstrosity. I thought that we had got rid of all those ugly pieces of junk described as art by the lunatics on the so-called arts department of the previous council. I just found another couple of pieces stuck on a traffic circle, it's a wonder there haven't been more accidents round there as drivers see that pile of garbage and lose concentration. I propose to the new board of Mere Folly that we stop wasting money on such garbage and use the money for more beneficial things.
Bert picked up his phone and phoned the new EA, 'Who is in charge of all this so-called art that is displayed around the City. Ok we will be over in thirty minutes to meet with her. Tell her to have a presentation ready. You know, lists photo's etc. Really, I don't care if she's busy, see you in thirty.'
I sometimes wonder if we did put the right person in charge, let's go.'
The boys walked through the reception area with Jim taking his usual time out to chat up the receptionist.
'When you've finished with him can you tell the EA that we are on our way up.'

Flustered, the receptionist, suddenly remembered what she was there for. 'The EA said to meet at the ground floor boardroom, where you will be joined by the director of art for the City.'

'The who, the what,' laughed Bert. 'When did that title arrive, I didn't know we had such an animal, I wonder what she does after the first five minutes of her day. I can't wait to meet this clown. By the way dear, who is the director of art.'

'Mary Moron,' smiled the receptionist.

The boys were besides themselves. "You've got to be bloody kidding, how long has she had that job, he's only been in the position for five minutes and already he is giving out sinecure jobs to his friends or in this case mistress,' said Kev.

Kev's blood was boiling as the boys walked into the boardroom. 'When were you going to fill us in on this special job,' he vented at the EA.

'What do you mean?'

'Why do we need somebody to buy pieces of junk to set around the City in the name of art?'

'Oh that.'

Kev's blood pressure was going higher, 'what do you mean? 'oh that' is this what you think that your new position is all about giving cushy numbers to your bloody mistress. To make it worse she is doing a lousy job as well,'

The EA hardly knew what to say. 'She has been doing this for about five years.'

'So, she is the one responsible for the crap on our riverbank and sidewalks, I didn't really understand the word ugly until I saw some of the stuff that she has put out there.'

Just then the door opened and in walked Mary Moron. The EA introduced her to the members of the sovereign state of Mere Folly ruling board. She shook their hands.

Tom spoke first, only to allow Kev to cool down and in case he blew a gasket. 'I see you have some photos on the ehmmm should we say items that have been purchased by the City over the past few years.'

After all the years the boys had been involved in the heartbeat of Mere Folly, this was the first time that they had really met and been up close and personal with her. Not in the same way that the Mayor now EA had been or is. As soon as she opened her mouth it was if the boys gained an instant dislike to her. There was something about her 'don't you know who I am' attitude and arrogance. She really didn't know who exactly the four seniors in the room were and immediately looked down on them.

'You are admirers of the art that I have purchased for the City then?'

The boys nearly fell off their seats.

Again, Tom stepped in before the board room imploded. 'Actually, we have the same opinion as many of the people who live in this City.'

She smiled.

Have you a price list and photographs of the various items?

'Why would you want to see that.'

That was too much for Bert to take. 'Would you like me to explain in words of no more than one syllable. This stuff is paid for by the citizens of Mere Folly, in lieu of the money going to health, social benefits, feeding the hungry and you want to hide it. Is the price list here

'No,' the moron hung her head realising that there could be some issues over the pieces that she had bought over the years. 'I will go and get it for you.' That confident arrogance had suddenly diminished somewhat.'

'Is it handy,' said Tom.

'What do you mean?'

'I will ask the EA's assistant to get it.'

'Pardon,' 'I think you heard me the first time. I will ask the EA's assistant to get it. Where do you keep it?'

'I will get it.'

'Didn't you hear me?'

'Don't you trust me? What do you think I am going to do with it? Eat it.'

'Yes, on both counts,' said Jim, 'now where do you keep it.'

The assistant was in and out in seconds, she could sense all was not well in the board room.

Jim, leafing through the file asked the moron where she got the stuff from. 'You can't just buy this crap, sorry art, at the local antique store, although looking at these photo's you probably can or if not at the local tip,'

By now the moron was losing it. 'who do you idiots think you are? I'm going to get you thrown out.'

'Hold on, hold on,' interrupted Bert, 'don't get your knickers in a twist, hasn't our illustrious EA here briefed you on the transition.'

'Well yes, we have all been briefed, what do you think we have been playing at for the past few weeks/'

'If you ask me,' said Kev, 'playing around with your knick-knacks. Just to get it through your thick head, we are the board of the sovereign state of Mere

Folly and it is our responsibility to make sure that this state is run properly. You might not like it but I am still trying to figure out what you do around here besides playing with your bits of rock as you pick up a nice fat salary. How and why were you kept on when the council was disbanded and its members let go? Don't answer that, I think I know the answer. Do you have a job description?'

The EA sat though this impassively, what could he say, he knew he was going to pay for it later. His mind was racing, this is what he wanted, her fired and out of the limelight and his life, but he was scared stiff in case she opened her mouth and started telling tales. Oh shit, he thought, I should have bumped her off when I first thought about it, how do I get out of this.

Jim carried on mooching through the file. 'Now I get it, you are good Mary, every piece of junk, I mean art that you bought for the City you got a cut of. Look at this, the invoice to you, $660,000, but this other company put on a 10% fee, so it actually cost the City $726,000, with the $66,000 going to this marketing company. You are dumb Mary, why use your name spelt backwards, Norom Marketing.'

Jim was back again, 'look where some of these pieces are from, Quebec. Why would you trade with Quebec? Can't you buy stuff like this locally or even from China at a tenth of the price. Here we are giving them all that money every year, subsidising them while we struggle to survive and you have the nerve to deal with them, paying outrageous prices for Quebec made junk. I would sooner see a 'Made in China' sticker on the junk at least we would know that we hadn't subsidised it and hadn't been fleeced. Look at this you even had the nerve, and you kept the newspaper article, to say that you had negotiated a ten per cent saving. If you hadn't of bought it you would have saved one hundred per cent. You are a nightmare

The EA and Mary Moron were in no mood for joviality, as Jim tore the file apart, the moron cringed.

However deep in Tom's mind was the feeling that they were creating an enemy. Sure, they could call in the police but the investigations and disturbance would create even more headaches. No, discretion was the better part of valour. He wanted it handled write now, leaving these two together would be dangerous, they could either kill each other or start opening their mouths.

I tell you what,' went on Tom, 'you two seem to get on together, why don't you Mary, work with the EA in administering Mere Folly.'

Bert, Jim and Kev looked at each other in astonishment. They had known Tom and his eccentricities for years, but this capped it. He can't be serious thought Bert. Under her breath, the moron breathed a sigh of relief. She had thoughts of the police being called in, this would give her a post in the City hierarchy and a chance to regroup. 'What if I don't accept the offer.'

Again, Jim, Bert and Kev looked at each other too shell shocked to stop Tom before he made matters any worse.

'I know that you have done some dumb things but you aren't that stupid,'

Our lawyers will draw up your contract and non-disclosure agreement, once signed, your first job will be to have all that crap that you bought removed.'

'What do you want me to do with it,' asked the moron.

'Do you really want us to answer that,' said Tom really enjoying himself. 'Try selling it, have a garage sale whatever, but get rid of it. Let's have an auction to get rid of this junk It will be interesting to see how much each piece goes for as compared to the price the City paid as he enjoyed the thought of the moron seething as the boys walked out of the room.

'Jim', said Tom, 'all is forgiven, you really are an HTSI, I thought that you have been pulling our legs all these years, now we have a 'Highly Trained Special Investigator' in our midst

The boys walked over to Chat, on the way Bert said to Tom,' I was wondering what you were up to and was expecting you to just fire them, but now I get it. If we had punted one or both of them, we would have had an enemy or enemies waiting in the weeds. Obviously, we don't trust them, I know it's a chance having them administering the City but at least we can keep an eye on them. We can gradually limit what they do until they won't even notice what they are not doing.'

'I wonder if those two will call in to Chat later,' said Tom.

'I doubt it, they will be beating each other up in bed in a few minutes,' said Kev.

They are welcome to each other, ugh the thought of it, I need that drink now' said Jim

Kev was right, well nearly, the EA and his new assistant or whatever title they could agree on were going for a drink, but the adrenalin was taking its toll.

'You sat there like a spare part, while they hammered me,' said the moron. "Why didn't you stand up for me, why didn't you tell me about those guys and who they were.

'You know as much as I do,' lied the EA.

'I was jealous after you had your fling with that slime ball from Toronto.'

Well who goes home to their wife every night?'

'I like it when you get worked up,' the EA could sense that sex was in the offing. 'Let's discuss it in bed.'

'Why not,' said the moron, 'guess who's out of town tonight?'

"It's been a long time my darling, said a breathless moron,'

'You haven't lost your appetite; you are still great at it.'

'Now that we can work together, we can go after those four idiots, gradually get rid of them and take over.'

Where have I heard that before mused the EA, but of course he knew on which side his bread was buttered and she was the last person he would trust.

'Come here;' he grasped her, but he couldn't make the bits work again so he went home to his wife.

Relief, when the EA got home, Mrs. EA wasn't there, then it dawned on him that she was out with her brood of hens. Peace perfect peace he said as he flopped down in a chair and flicked on the television.

Mrs. EA sat with her friends over dinner, perhaps not friends but people she had known over a period of years. They got together on each other's birthday and as the EA would say, to talk each other to death. It used to drive the Mayor nuts because when she came home from one of those gatherings she would bitch, complain, want to do something or want something. It's as if the whole brood had been playing one up woman ship all evening.

'We never watch movies, they do, they were talking about movies that had seen on TV I don't get the chance to watch movies you don't let me have the movie channels you are too tight to pay for the channels.'

Movie channels, delightful he thought. That must have been the topic of conversation, I suppose that's cheaper than new kitchens or world cruises. He sat there wishing he could get rid of her as she blabbed on. If I won the lottery, I would give her half, no three quarters, leave her to her own devices and go and buy a place in the sun, she probably wouldn't even know I was gone.

Later in bed, she was on again that she wanted the movie channels, 'All my friends have the movie channels,' she moaned.

'You never watch movies you watch the house decorating and house selling shows. We had Netflix for a time, but you never watched it, you said the movies weren't intellectual enough for you.'

'It shows you what you know. The movie channels show a better class of movie which is what I need to stimulate my intellect.'

How can you stimulate a cretin? he thought to himself as he pulled the sheets over his head to shut out the light and the noise.

CHAPTER 8.

The launch of the Mere Folly insurance program went down very well. In keeping with the philosophy of having no offices downtown, the head office was set up in one of the business parks with a couple of sub offices dotted around the outskirts. The internet distribution network became the hub of the enterprise. Greg was loving his new job with his ideas on specialty financial products introduced bit by bit. When people from outside the sovereign state saw the program, especially the pricing, they wanted to buy their insurance in Mere Folly, but to no avail. The board was adamant that no outsiders could join the program, it was for the benefit of Mere Folly citizens only

We are not interested in commercial insurance either, the prices are too low and of course all the brokers and insurers actually think that commercial insurance has some kudos, even though these entities lose money for them. Let's face it there is an easy way to grind down the premium on your commercial insurance. You go to your other broker and tell him what you are paying. He will come back with a lower premium. Then you go back to your broker and tell him that you have been quoted an even lower price. You could do this a few times and eventually you will save a chunk on your premium. Make sure that you get the final cheaper price from your existing broker. Then you go back to him and tell him that for the past how many years he and his insurers have been ripping you off. Therefore, you would like the five years additional premium that it has cost you being loyal to him back.

Then you go to your broker and ask him to explain what all the additional frills and liability coverage means that you have on your policy, you pick on the ones you don't need and ask why you need them. For instance, 'brands and labels', why do you need that cover when you don't produce a product? If you don't need it why do you have to pay for it, therefore can you have the premium that you have been paying for it for the past years back.

There will be casualties, the insurance offices of the brokers and direct writers. The Insurance companies really didn't care as the volume of business that they lost in Mere Folly was drop in the bucket compared to their writings as a whole. Brokers and Insurers offices moved out of the City, they were losing all their home and auto business to the program. The brokers wanted to market and administer the program but couldn't or wouldn't agree on a commission rate so Greg hired their good local people to work at the MF Insurance Company head and sub offices. Once the Company was moving along and the boys were able to attract the good people that they knew could do a job. As the boys discussed, none of this advertising, interviewing and personality testing garbage. They knew the good, the bad and the ugly and those that could do the job from their years of working with and around them.

    The sovereign city state of Mere Folly soon became the centre of insurance experience and expertise, with Greg leading the way with his specialty products that were needed by and of benefit to the general public. MF Insurance Company was growing profitably with its base of local customers to become a national writer of small premium, low exposure, service orientated quality insurance.

The number of resumes flowing to the Company grew, the quality of applicants increased, the big brokers came banging on the door for contracts. MFIC employees didn't need licensing why would they.

Greg was invited to a national insurance conference to speak. 'You are diluting the quality of the insurance industry, by regulating it to death. Compliance has become a sub industry; it doesn't care about consumers as it's a self-serving industry looking for self-preservation and mass production. Why has an insurance company where the underwriters have to be licensed but not the claims staff? How is it that a person with no insurance experience can get a licence allowing he or she within a month to step into a job with the full authority to advise clients with multi-million-dollar risks on how they should have their risk insured. Then the person that he or she reports to with forty years of experience has to go to him or her to get permission to write a risk. Ladies and Gentlemen no wonder the insurance industry is grouped with realtors and car salesmen as the most disliked people to deal with. Thank goodness I don't have to deal with regulators and insurance councils any more, that's why we are so successful. He then walked out the door to a standing ovation, with the regulators that were there, totally bemused. When he got back to Mere Folly the social media was adulatory. The regulators were getting rather incensed as Greg and the boys were confirming what most of the industry knew. These organizations were run by people with their own agenda and mostly manned by people that had never worked in the industry and those that had were only there because nobody else would hire them. The regulators, being arrogant and besotted with power, let's face it, the powers that be in the industry gave up fighting the regulators, even though they were right, as they hadn't got the time.

However, over a celebratory dinner, the consensus was that it is the industry's problem, it's up to them to either keep the status quo or do something about it. In the meantime, we will prosper while we run the organization to benefit our policy holders, and not the regulators.

The big city to the south was also prospering, well its hotels were. The board of Mere Folly had no intention of allowing more hotels to be built so visitors be they tourists or on business had to stay outside of Mere Folly. It was only twenty minutes away and hotels were springing up literally over-night. In fact, hotels competing for business were running shuttles.

As part of the MFIC reinsurance negotiations, the boys and Greg were invited over to the so-called mecca of the insurance world London.

Flying used to be such a pleasure, courteous staff, edible food, comfortable seats, even in cattle class. The country's national airline as Bert said has everybody by the balls. The boys hated travelling from the big city 'international' airport notwithstanding the fact that it had fallen out with most international carriers it made it virtually impossible to fly anywhere outside of the country direct.

'This is a pain,' You have to go through the hassle of changing planes to get out of the damn country,' said Jim, 'why can't we get a direct flight from here? It's a city of a million people. It's not our fault that the airport people and the airlines can't get on with each other.'

'You are missing the real reason guys,' said Greg. See all these eateries and bars they have built. That's the reason. They want you to spend your money on inflated pricey food and booze. Then when you get on the plane you won't mind missing their garbage food. Then when you change planes you have more time to kill and spend more money

The boys got off the first plane and made their way through the newly constructed terminal with its little cars taxying them to the gates.

'This is neat' said Jim at least they have got something right

As they made their way through the melee of lost souls trying to figure out which way the should go, it was obvious that the person that designed the gate access had probably never flown cattle class. Passengers were standing in in line, no seats standing room only, there was still ninety minutes to go before the plane was to leave. Jim saw that and suggested that they go for a coffee, 'they are not going to give our seats away and I'm not going to stand in line for an hour.'

'Told you said Greg, another way to get your money off you. I reckon that the airline got fed up with all the people crowding around the desk even though they are asked by the staff to wait until their row or zone is called. Payback time, if you want to stand and wait, we will make you stand and wait, but on our terms.'

The boys had their coffee walked past the line of frustrated passengers on their way to the premium gate. All any passenger wanted to do was to get on the plane, sit down and relax, but they were made to go through the final torment and frustration of standing and waiting.

'This is what makes laugh,' said Bert, 'virtually everybody has their baggage with them, look at that guy, he has three bags. Why do the airlines tell you that carry-on bags are limited by number and size? That guy obviously never went anywhere near the bag size frame. If they check bags prior to getting on board it's going to be hours before the plane leaves. I don't get it.'

'If I get banged by another bag,' said Bert, 'look they can hardly get them down the aisle. Look at it a mess of carry-on bags squeezing down the aisles banging and upsetting other passengers as they try to heave their bags into inadequate bins. Are you sure that you are restricted to the size and number of bags you bring on board, its apparent that nobody has told the staff?'

'It defies logic,' said Tom. 'They charge to put bags in the hold so people bring them on board. Why not charge extra for bags taken on board and let the bags going in the hold go for free?

'Don't be silly,' said Jim, 'that's common sense, the airlines will never go with that,' as a lady swung her bag round and knocked his glass of water out of his hand.

Jim mopped up the water, as a stewardess cast a miserable glance at him and let him get on with it, thanks for your help he said under his breath. 'She's all mirth and happiness, isn't she?'

They realized that they were stuck with the same miserable flight attendants for the next nine or so hours on a freezing plane. People were putting their coats on, kids were crying.

'Why don't they turn the heat up? Do they have to stick money in a meter? Asked Kev.

He asked the stewardess to turn up the heat, but fifteen minutes later he realized that his request was ignored. The kids were still crying and people were huddled under their coats.

Kev had had enough and got out of seat to find the stewardesses having a laugh and a joke in their little kitchen. He was very polite, unusual for Kev in such circumstances, he suggested that if they put the heat up then as the kids were cold, they would get warmer, stop crying and go to sleep. The stewardess gave him a nasty glare and wandered off, the heat went on, people relaxed and babies stopped crying.

In London the crowd going through customs was never ending but they seemed to move freely, the customs people although stern, were well mannered and friendly and there at the carousel the bags were waiting.

The boys' contact in London told them a car would pick them up and drop them at the hotel. 'After that flight, all we need is the car not to turn up,' said a weary Jim. 'I could do with getting my head down.'

'Worst thing you could do' said Bert, 'as he spotted a sign attached to a smartly dressed man's hand reading MF. 'Well I presume that's us, if it isn't the other MF will be a bit upset.'

After a brief car rid through central London, the boys checked in, managed not to go to bed, wandered down to the river, had a few beers, a meal and then back to the hotel to bed.

'That was a night on the town' laughed Tom at breakfast the next morning. 'How did you sleep Jim.'

'Great, in between staring at the ceiling and watching TV.'

The meetings in the City went well, in and out of the various buildings, Lloyds, the Gherkin, the Walkie Talkie and the Cheese Grater. Up and down in high speed lifts, hardly any board room meetings most were in lounges high up in the buildings overlooking the city through glass walls. Sat in comfy chairs or on couches with a cappuccino or latte served from little coffee bars visiting the many insurers and financial entities that were interested and showed an appetite for doing business in Mere Folly. By the time the three days of visits and meetings had finished they had their patter of to a fine art and sounded like parrots as they explained to the various parties who they were, their experience and their story in general.

One thing was gnawing away at Tom, so when he had the chance, he asked Allen, one of the broker team they were working with. 'During the meetings one theme that kept coming up was compliance, why is everybody over here scared stiff of it? It's become a quasi-industry all on its own, a money pit for regulators and government departments All it does is create jobs and make insurance more expensive.'

'You are right,' said George, we have a few minutes, on the way to lunch let's take a short cut, I want to show you something to confirm your thinking.'

They were taken to the main insurance building, up, on the seventh floor, they were in a room the size of a football pitch, it was jammed with humanity hammering away at computer keyboards with hardly any room between them.

'Wow.' Said Bert, it's a modern sweatshop, this compliance really is serious stuff over here.'

As they walked through the City to go to lunch, they sidestepped the crowds of suits stood outside the pubs.

'No wonder it's difficult to do business with people involved with the industry here, they are all stood on the sidewalks drinking beer,' said Jim.

After lunch on the way to another meeting, Jim was in his element, 'Look they are still here and I'm sure that's not the same pint. I like my beer and wine as much as the next person, but if I drank as much as they do, I would have to take every afternoon off.'

'They probably do,' said Tom, 'that's why you can never get hold of them.'

After a week of cappuccino's, nice lunches, lavish dinners, a football match, the boys were at Heathrow with its hugely populated airport security moving smoothly and quickly. The staff were pleasant and again well mannered, a far cry from where they had come from where they are miserable and obviously don't want to be working there. The plane was there waiting; walked straight through and sat down. Actually, the food was quite edible the flight quite pleasant compared to the one going out.

The obligatory change of planes with the usual rush to customs, a long wait to meet the most miserable customs people on earth.

'What a way to welcome visitors,' said Kev, 'I have actually met tourists who have vowed never to come again due to the nasty customs officials. They should take a look at their counterparts in other countries, they might learn something, such as politeness and manners. '

Another even longer wait; this time for the 'puddle jumper' to take them the forty-five minutes to their home airport. Of course, the airline staff had to tow the line and board all fifty passengers by the book, or in this case by zone. Not by row number boarding from the back first to make it easier getting up and down the aisle but by zone, which in essence is the equivalent of trying to fit a bunch more things into a fully stuffed suitcase.

'We're in zone 1' said Kev, first on at the front,'

'Perfect,' thought Bert, 'then you have everybody with their bags hitting and banging you as they make their way to the back.'

As they led the way through the door to make their way to the tarmac the airline staff forgot to tell them that we would be travelling to the plane by bus. Therefore, when the bus arrived at the plane, the boys knowing that they had the four front seats stood back and watched the chaos ensue, the orderly embarkation by zone or row had gone by the board, it was absolute carnage as the passengers, bags and other accompaniments took part in the usual free for all to get on the plane first. It didn't matter that everybody had a specific seat and of course nobody explained that the plane wouldn't be going until everybody was on board. Those who had got on first and sat in an aisle seat had to try to get up to let the person with the window seat in. Once the chaos had abated, the boys wandered on the plane and took their seats.

'Never again,' said Bert. 'Never again.'

As everybody finally calmed down and waited for the plane to leave, the pilot came on the inter com and apologized for the fact that passengers had to be bussed to the plane and then went on to say that with all the millions spent the developing the airport the designers would have thought about building bays for all planes using the airport.

Stunned silence, except for Bert muttering away, 'Never again, never again.'
It was only a forty-five-minute flight in a cigar tube so who cared about refreshments. Well not the passengers, they just wanted to get off the perishing plane.

Kev was tired and half asleep when the stewardess offered him snacks. 'Who the hell cares about a glass of water and some pretzels.'

Most people refused, so why bother on such a short flight. In these days of airline austerity surely, it's not worth the expense, it would also save the staff the aggravation of having to get out a clapped-out old trolley which had seen better times and push it up and down an aisle dodging people's elbows.

After standing around at the carousel for an hour, Jim had to admit that he now understood why people went through the hassle and irritation of taking their bags on board. 'I bet they only have two people working on baggage handling and we have landed right in the middle of their coffee break. This airport now has my vote as the worst airport in the world. How is it that airports like Heathrow with literally thousands of bags continuously arriving all the time can have your bags ready and waiting for you, yet this dump with the odd plane and a few bags arriving every now and again can't deliver. That's it, this airport can't deliver, period.'

Other than their jaunt through their local airport, the trip was a real success, in a very short time coupled with its geographical position, the sovereign state of

Mere Folly was becoming a centre within the insurance and financial industry.

CHAPTER 9.

The boys were sat by the canal savouring their wine when out of the blue one of the them, who had been kind of out of it with his mind on other things, asked if they ever think about their past and whether they sometimes wish that they could turn back the clock.
'Why would you do that, we've probably got everything we could have ever dreamed of. Look at it all, this is ours and there is much more ahead.'
'I know but, remember the judge and how he got back with his first love then they sailed off into the sunset? I don't know what happened but it triggered the memory of my first love. Mind you, over the years there isn't a day, week or so that goes by when I don't think about her, where she's at, what she's doing. I am for ever thinking about her.
'Grow up, even if you did find her how many years ago did you two last see each other?'
About forty, fifty years or so ago.'
'You've got to be kidding, she could be dead.'
'As we have discussed many times, it's the tale of the tape and if you have the opportunity, go for it. You can't put the clock back so you must seize the chance when it confronts you. Look at the judge as an example, look how happy he seems to be, go for it, what have you got to lose. What's the worst that can happen, she either doesn't remember you or tells you to leave her alone. Go for it, what have you got to lose, if you don't, you'll for ever be thinking about her and regret it for the rest of your life.'

Life's too short so seize the opportunity. This had become their mantra and been the driving force behind the development of their companies and then Mere Folly.

'Here we are a bunch of hard-nosed seniors telling you to put some romance in your life. Go for it perhaps you will get some fun and joy out of your final years. You probably won't find her, but if you do and the door opens that's when you start making decisions, not now. Great thing the internet, go for it.'

A week later, three of them were already in Chat when the other arrived smiling. 'Read this.' What do I do now?

"Hi, of course I remember you! You were my first love! Ahh how sweet! We were all of 15/16 I think!"

'Wow! now it is decision time. I don't know why she's still interested in you, but there's fire somewhere and obviously, from what you say you've never fallen out of love with her.'

He didn't say much that afternoon; he was debating whether to really open up or keep any progress under wraps for now. He was anxious and didn't want to be seen as an old fool, but even at his age he knew he was in love with her again. The boys left him alone sensing he had other things on his mind. Eventually, it was decided, to ask the leading question.

'Are you two actually going to talk to each other?'

He surprised them all, he wanted someone to share his good fortune with, he wanted to reveal his excitement.

'Don't laugh, here me out. We have been in touch but haven't spoken to each other yet. We have been going backwards and forwards catching up trying to remember and piece together our initial time together. We started to recount our early lives, literally simultaneously, backwards and forwards, how we met and what happened.

'This is getting serious, carry on.'

'All of a sudden the boys' character changed, strangely they became more perceptive.

'If you aren't your usual bloody sarcastic selves and can remain serious, I would love to fill you in.

'I was always thinking about her. Remember that Moody Blues song 'Somewhere?" I came across it and now can't get it out of my head, I should send it to her.

After getting the encouragement from you guys, I knew it was a long shot, but why not just type her name in Google? Lo and behold! There she was, a Manager at a University. I wrote to her and she wrote back!

'Hi, of course I remember you! You were my first love! Ahh how sweet we were all of 15/16 I think!'

Most mornings, around 9.30 the boys would meet in the Vineyard cafe for a coffee, discuss the previous day's events, review their operations and generally put their world and the rest of the world to rights.

As they sat down, it was noticeable. 'You look pretty pleased with yourself; I hope that this is for real now.

'I'm in with a chance, look She has sent me a photograph! Those eyes, she is still beautiful.'

'Hold on, hold on, you sound like you were sixteen again. I am sure that she is happily married and again wants to carry on her own life.'

He ignored that comment. 'I can't help but wonder why she would even respond if she wasn't interested?'

The first thing I do upon getting up is to get to the computer. When there is no message, I am so disappointed it virtually ruins my day. I would even put off coffee until after 10 a.m., by then it was 5pm over there and would have left her office. After that first week I thought that that was the end, nothing. The weekend was intolerable, a short-lived romance, but I was determined not to be a prick and keep bugging her.

Then elation as Monday arrived with a message, a brief, "Sorry it was hectic when I got back from Germany and then to cap it, I was off work with a bug. I am only working mornings at the moment".

So that's why nothing had happened while I was sat at that computer. By the time I was organised she was long gone. Then she educated me in the world of new age communication, we started to talk on What's App.

'Well it's taking her a long time, its Tuesday and you being the patient guy that you are, I want to believe that perhaps she does care as much as you do. Why not make this happen? You might as well take the bull by the horns; it's gnawing away at you. At your age you need to get your act together and concentrate on your other responsibilities, you are behaving like a romantic love- struck teenager anyway, so why don't you get real and go for it.'

'This is how I felt about Her when I was fifteen and sixteen and nineteen or twenty. It's a cliché, but I have never felt like this about anyone else. I wish she would realise, but I can't make her. She has a life far away from me.'

'Exactly, you live your life, let her live her life and more importantly we have an update meeting with the newspaper guys in thirty minutes.'

The boys were bemused and still laughing, they couldn't grasp how an attractive woman would remember and want to renew the romance that she had with this friend of theirs. They knew him far better than she did, he was a great guy, but to her a stranger that had a schoolboy/teenage crush on her?'

Much to the surprise of the boys, the texts continued, backwards and forwards as he kept them updated. As in the case of the judge, even though they weren't into romance, true love and all that kind of slush, the boys were thrilled that hopefully he had found the girl of his dreams and could regain his composure.

"Her" - "Funny how someone you haven't heard from for years can take up so much of your thoughts!"

"Him"- "Now you know how I feel - we really didn't get to know each other did we

"Her" - "No not at all really, a lifetime has passed since then! Oooh too deep - I'm going home now definitely before I start to feel decrepit! CU!

He decided that he didn't want to bore the boys, so he kept his mouth shut. He was on a roll with Her.

If they wanted to bring the matter up, then so be it. He wasn't going to wait for Her e mail, he didn't care whose turn it was, so he started writing, politely, and then it just started developing and flowing. Why sit on the fence. Try to make something happen. Saying what he thought and how he felt. All of a sudden, a pang of uncertainty crept in, he pondered and wrestled as to whether to send it. He decided not to send it but to wait. Then he made a few changes, even adding a note of apology at the beginning. Blow it, he had to know and pressed the send button. It stayed in the outbox for ever. Why? was it a coincidence? An e mail came in. Perhaps that was a warning, was it a get out clause, a safety valve telling him not to send it! He had to know, he didn't want to lose her, he had to know. Should he have waited? He wasn't known for his patience. Should he switch things around, get desperate and come to you. Blow that, he was too fond of her to let that bother him. Perhaps she would understand he needed to know!

Sitting there, staring into his cappuccino, the other three were deep in conversation on the business of the day. If She had responded with "Go to hell!" he wouldn't have been happy, but he would have known. Should he telephone her? Should he leave a message that he was concerned as to whether she had received his e mails. He was on a mission! Typical, the dreaded voicemail. Why don't people just say 'leave a message,' instead of making you wait while they drivel on. He knew who she was, that she wasn't there and when she did, he would leave his message. I'll get back to you as soon as I can" Here goes! "Hi, sorry to bother you. I didn't know whether my e mails were getting through, are you were still sick or in Europe somewhere singing.

Now I've contacted you, even if it is by plastic voice mail, I'll relax and leave the ball in your court. If I don't hear from you, I will appreciate that and understand why. Take care."

Over coffee, one of the guys made the mistake of asking Him how his serial romance was going. The others yawned as He carried on. 'I couldn't sleep, only dream. It hurt, but what could I do. I'd pushed it as far as I could.'

This wasn't the guy that they had grown old with, he was turning into a blubbering wreck.

'You could always fly over, find out one way or another, anything so that we can get some bloody peace.'

'What should I do? Can you imagine, walking into her office and saying "Hi",

As far as I know my credibility is about zero with her. Any more and I would be getting a call from her husband, lawyer and be accused of stalking. Even Guido with his violin case could pop by! This has affected my whole life. Maybe I should change my life completely, I could go somewhere and start again with her.'

His phone beeped as an e mail arrived.

"Her" - I don't know why I didn't carry on with the emails before when I contacted you. I obviously wasn't ready to make more of the situation. Perhaps I shouldn't have got in touch when I saw your name on the website, it was just those memories again. Recently married again and a new grand-daughter on the scene I obviously had other things on my mind and I couldn't see the point when you were "so far away". I was to find out how much that song would be part of my life years later! Now it's great to hear from you again and quite a surprise! At first. I thought "That's nice". A bit of innocent flirting does you good what is the phrase "you can look at the menu as long as you don't sample it!" I didn't think it was anything other than fond reminiscences. But it came to mean more than this and I was enjoying the attention from you! My memories of you were always good and visions of a lost love were never far away. It became evident that you weren't just flirting; I think you actually mean it! Panic, hold back! Ok never mind you're out of harm's way, it's a long way. You were "so far away". I couldn't get that song out of my mind. Then I got your message on the voice mail oh no! Getting in a bit deep here I think I had better cool it, you are obviously looking for more than I can give and I don't want to give you any false hopes. I miss you now; I look forward to your emails! The feelings are still there! Are you going to London! Shall we meet up? It's on! It's off! You are saying that you don't want to compromise me and that we shouldn't meet in London after all. I'm disappointed at that, we were never very good at getting it together, perhaps it's for the best, what if I go shopping and I meet you for lunch it's silly not to after all these years! We seem to be getting very close with our texts and I look forward to opening my home and work emails to read your words, perhaps too much. Things are hotting up and Aunty Mary keeps telling me, "be very careful!" I have stopped telling her about the emails and comment casually if she asks, confirming that we are still in touch. Shall we take it one step further and you visit. Should I stay overnight? A room of my own in London, how nice and very proper but you know that I wouldn't go without this arrangement.

The boys were absorbed, this is getting serious, are you really going to visit her?'

'Yes, I am, I have to find out if we are an item again. I'll only be gone a week or so.

At first, He was reading Her e mails to the boys, but now, as matters were getting far more serious, He would just keep them updated. Enough to keep them in the picture but not enough that they knew how seriously this relationship was developing.

He got up to another e mail. 'Thanks for sending me the CD, the songs the 'meaningful words! I play it all the time in my car; it's a long time since I felt a glow and feelings like this! I am going to make plans to go to London on a 'telecommunications' seminar, well I do go to Imperial College sometimes! I have to tell my friend and colleague I usually go to these 'do's' with that I am meeting an 'old boyfriend' for lunch just in case she sees the Prof. Just a one off I say, a quick lunch and then I'm off shopping! Another warning to be careful! Hey Ho!

"Her" the decision is made. We start counting the days to our meeting and getting very excited! 14 sleeps! Then 3 then 1! I've also made a CD for Him, we have become close over the internet and occasional phone calls and I have included songs I wouldn't have thought possible a few weeks ago, I hope I haven't been too forward. If we don't get on I needn't give it to him anyway! Waiting for the train at the station and I'm really excited I feel quite naughty but much empowered with my new feelings! We talk on the phone while I'm on the train – I am so nervous! Are we doing the right thing here? We might get on too well – or we might not like each other when we are face to face again – I can't really imagine that though! The train is pulling in! Here we go! Oh, where has my stomach gone! There he is, standing at the barrier – he hasn't changed! My legs are like jelly.

"Him" - A tap on my back as I stared intently at the masses of passengers coming off the platforms. When you actually see your first love after months of planning and forty years of waiting, my heart just melted - it's a moment I will never forget. A big hug – a kiss on the cheek, hardly captures the moment. How was the trip I mumbled? I can't remember what She said. Her eyes are exactly the same, of course they had to be – but was she still the same, only time would tell. I knew it though, as soon as I saw her. There was still something between us. I had gone from the east London version of a hotel by Tower Bridge, grabbed a cab to the hotel in Knightsbridge. We had planned this and I booked it with my points. Two rooms. Determined that I didn't want this construed as a dirty weekend, I just wanted to be accepted by her as a sign of respect for her. It must be awfully difficult, spending a few days with an ex – boyfriend she hardly knew. I even checked in to the hotel first, had my bags delivered to the rooms, chose the largest room for Her, with the king-sized bed, nothing can go wrong. At the time I didn't even think about the relevance of a king-sized bed in our relationship. The man bringing the cases winked at me and said that if I wanted the adjoining door open, there would be no problem, just call housekeeping. Did I look that eager? As I went through the hotel lobby, I felt good. It was a nice hotel. Nice rooms and it appeared to be nicely organized for my Cat. Cat short for catalyst. She was the catalyst for our love. She was the inspiration. I left her for a while and unpacked. I knocked on her door, couldn't wait to be with her again. We talked- almost incessantly and when we didn't, we reminded ourselves of our youth. She was so natural, we figured out what we were going to do. Harrods first and we held hands as we walked up the Knightsbridge Road! In Harrods we actually walked around the food hall, and bought lunch to take away and eat somewhere. We walked and found a beautiful rose garden in Hyde Park and a bench on which to sit while we ate our sandwiches. This was a first for us. We talked as we had promised to do about our respective situations. We were both brutally honest with each other. There was no other way. We walked we talked, getting to know each other again. By Green Park we caught the sightseeing bus, joked with the driver – no inhibitions, we were happy.

"Her" I realized I couldn't go through the barrier with my e ticket so I contrived to dodge his gaze and sneaked around to the side gate and around the back! I tapped him on the shoulder and he beamed at me! My heart flipped! We hugged, a quick kiss and it was strange! We quickly composed ourselves and walked off to get a taxi to the hotel as if we'd done it many times before! The hotel was really nice and it felt right being there with him. I smiled to myself as we walked in when the doorman exchanged looks with Him, he seemed very confident and it put me at my ease. We unpacked quickly and got back together as soon as we could, I felt sure that we both didn't want to waste a moment! He had said that he liked looking round Harrods so off we went (me noticing immediately that Harvey Nicholls was next door to the hotel!) hand in hand. Harrods was fun we walked around looking at all the fabulous food and bought our lunch there. I wanted to look at the Egyptian foyer and the escalator that had been made to look like a pyramid, it was great, we wandered around looking at the antique jewellery and then went off to find somewhere to eat our lunch. We walked along Rotten Row where all the posh people used (and some still do) to ride their horses and dress up in their carriages! We found a perfect bench under an arbour of roses and got closer. We talked and talked, we never gave ourselves this opportunity before, we knew so little about each other then and we were so naive. It all came easily and I began to relax and became really glad that we had arranged to meet. He kissed me there on the bench, a tentative kiss but just as good as I had hoped it would be. There were to be more of those gentle kisses that afternoon!

We caught the tour bus and sat as close as we could, it was great to see London from the open top bus but I was so aware of him sitting next to me and the feeling was great! We stayed on as long as we could and then went to the embankment and drank a jug of Pimm's on a boat on the Thames, perfect! Time to get back to the hotel to shower

and change for our big date! We walked all the way and we were quite tired especially Him who had had a busy few days and a long flight before he met me.

"Him" I don't know where I kissed Her for the first time, wish I could remember, but it was magical. The burning question. Was she doing this to make me happy? I soon learned that she was enjoying it as much as me and would tell me straight out if she had any concerns! Back to the Hotel, into our own separate rooms. I had a power nap, then a shower. Really nice showers. Knock on the door. She saying that she was ready. She looked gorgeous. I rushed to get ready, obviously wanted to look OK! Knocked on her door. She looked wonderful. I was very proud to walk through the hotel with her on my arm. We caught a cab to the restaurant. The meal was really good. I felt so relaxed with her, she was a natural. A beautiful special person to be with. We humoured the waiters; the meal was excellent. But just being with Her gave it the ambience it made the evening. She is a very classy lady. How I wish that I could take her to dinners and functions etc. on a regular basis. The Gigondas was good, and then we shared a desert. We walked back to the hotel, talking, holding hands, the odd kiss, we were becoming a couple. I wish I could remember where I first told Her that I loved her and where she told me she loved me.

"Her" - I went straight into the shower, I didn't want to keep him waiting! All spruced up and I thought I'd better knock his door in case he was ready but just giving me more time. He wasn't ready! He had snatched 40 winks clever boy and he was raring to go after a shower. We got a cab to the Restaurant, it looked very nice and staff seemed friendly, not too stiff so we chose our meal and relaxed with each other. I can't remember what conversation led us to our declaration but we told each other that we still had feelings for each other and shared the Love word! A lovely meal in perfect company and I was walking on air back to the hotel!

"Him' - To Her room - We listened to the CD She had compiled for me and she brought Out the port. I had asked her to bring me a bottle back from Portugal, she forgot. Not this time though. We sat next to each other on the couch. Looking at each other. Her with her gorgeous eyes. We kissed, held each other. We were in the hotel room, there was the king-sized bed. What do you think that I had promised myself? No way would I even attempt anything. We talked about how we both felt at that time. Perhaps we should have let our feelings drive us. We are both glad that we didn't. There is a natural respect and a bond growing between us. I forced myself out of that room! When I got into bed I thought and then phoned Her under the pretext of saying goodnight. Makes me laugh now, but afterwards I felt like a real clown as soon as I put the phone down. That was pretty classless.

"Her" - We went to my room and I gave Him the port I had brought with me, a small bottle just right to finish off the evening listening to the CD I had made for him. There was no doubt that we were going to take this relationship further the electric between us was evident and we both felt it. I wanted to be with Her completely that night it had been so special but I knew it wasn't right we shouldn't rush it and perhaps regret it, never! He was a star and he made himself go back to his room; I think he had more will power than me that night I don't think I would have said no. He phoned to say goodnight and I wanted to say "come back" but I'm so glad I didn't as the whole thing, waiting and getting to know him was so exciting.

"Him" - Next morning I was up and showered, dressed. I knocked on Her door. She was still in her pyjamas. We kissed again; I was so tempted. Now I know She was as well. However, we gritted our teeth and didn't succumb. We were getting to know each other more day by day and every time I had her in my arms and we kissed I just melted. We found a little café for breakfast, sitting with her and thinking was great. Toast, orange juice and coffee were never this good. The atmosphere is so different in Europe. On to Harvey Nicholls. Showing me the expensive shoes etc. shopping was Great with her must be in love to admit that. We looked for sunglasses, every pair I tried on She laughed at me. Then I found a pair and was frightened by the price, so I did without. We caught the bus again, we wanted to go to Tower Bridge, but the bus went the wrong way and took longer than we had anticipated. On the ride I was trying to guess what She would like best. Simple things such as should we get on or off the bus weighed heavily. Eventually we made it. Tower Bridge that is. Went down to the boardwalk south of the Thames by the bridge. We sat outside a café and had a quick lunch with a glass of wine, just talked – it was great. She really is wonderful!

"Her" the next morning He knocked my door but I was still in my PJ's! He came in and we could hardly keep our hands off each other but again we were good and I had a cold shower! We wandered down the High Street and found a nice café for breakfast. Breakfast at Tiffany's couldn't have been better! We looked into each other's eyes and went a bit shy again for a while! We went to Harvey Nicholls and quickly out again, a bit too pricy for this occasion! Off to get the bus again and headed for Tower Bridge, today we were going on the London Eye, I was really looking forward to it. We got on the bus going the wrong way and I wondered if we were ever going to get there! I had lost my bearings but it was OK and we enjoyed more holding hands and closeness on the open top bus. He had been along this part of the river before and we found a nice place for a 'lite lunch' – can't undo all my good work! We grabbed a cab on The Bridge and he took us to the Eye for our 3.00 PM booking. My phone rang! It Andrew to tell me he was getting his Op on Monday, Oh, how embarrassing, I hope He doesn't think I'm heartless! One of the guys at work had told me not to worry about the queues at the Eye as they went down quickly. It was great, first in the pod and our own spot to look all around. We had our photo taken and we both took a copy – I thought it was a good photo of both of us and I wanted a reminder that we had really been together!

"Him" - I could have sat and talked all day, but we had to be at the eye – which we both were looking forward to. We started to walk over Tower Bridge; our minds must have been somewhere else as we didn't realize how long it would take us. When you look west and can't see the eye you know it's a long walk. A cab came by fortunately he stopped and we climbed over the barrier. Her phone went – Andrew - I looked away. Still felt embarrassed. Why should I – I think that I respected and appreciated her more. Good job we grabbed the taxi or else we would have still been walking. We made it in time but those little adversities only helped us to laugh and joke. The eye was one big line up, normally I would be paranoid. We didn't care.

The eye was great, we talked laughed and we enjoyed each other's company – it was if we had known each other for years. It was so relaxing and natural; we were at the front of the pod as we came in to "land" and had our photo taken. She bought the photos one each, the two of us together. Everything seemed to go right. The worst moment. We realized that our trip was at an end. That walk through the park, past Buckingham Palace to the hotel. We even saw Andre Agassi on the way. That's how it was we talked, we laughed and we joked, we were so in love. We picked up the bags at the hotel and took a taxi to Marylebone Station where 2 days ago we didn't really know each other but what a difference now. The trip back, poignant, nothing lasts for ever, especially the good times. So lucky, we found two seats by ourselves at the back of the carriage and slotted the big case behind us. We sat in those 2 seats and talked, we kissed. I told Her that I loved her. It wasn't the first time but it was right it was so good. She told me she loved me which really made my heart melt. On those two seats at the back of the carriage we really talked openly. What we meant to each other. Although I was hoping that She felt the same way about me as I felt about her – this was the time when I really knew that we had a mutual relationship – we didn't want the train ride to ever end. The station came far too soon. She drove me to a relative's house in her car. We stopped at the bottom of the street like two discreet lovers. We agreed to meet at the local shops at 2 the next day. We walked back to the hotel through the park, I took a photo of the changing of the guard and we saw Andre Agassi coming out of a posh hotel! Our trip was nearly over and although we had said that we might catch the later train we sensibly went for the

17.05 as planned. We were both tired, not just from the 2 days but the accumulation of emotions too – it was for me anyway and He is usually feeling the same as me - I think we are a matched pair! I wished the train ride would never end, we managed surreptitious kisses and held each other close all the way home not wanting to let go. We found the car and I drove him to his relative's house. Andrew phoned to see where I was but I had a good excuse not to answer while I was driving. Worrying that we might be seen was a new one for me and I was very worried at that stage as we were so close to the house and I didn't want us to set tongues wagging! I hadn't been sure whether I would see Him when he got to town as I knew he had family commitments to attend to so I was thrilled when he suggested that we could meet the next day. We agreed to meet at the local shops when I finished work and off I went to Andrew – he was agitated about his op and I felt a bit guilty – but only a bit!

"Him" - Weeks before I was hoping that we could meet after the London trip, even for a coffee. It was happening I was in seventh heaven and didn't want to ever say goodbye to Her All Friday morning I was waiting. Waiting for 2pm to come along, it couldn't come too soon. I would have walked down to the shops myself, but I had to invent a story that I was meeting an old school friend. My cousin George offered to drive me, why don't we go for a beer on the way? I really wasn't bothered but he wanted to talk. So, I got the potted story of his version of his marriage breakdown. All I was concerned about was being at the shops at 2pm for Her We parked at the roadside. He hung around, and then said he had to go to the bank. This was right where Her and I were meeting. Just then who should park right behind George but Her. Can you believe it! "I Hope that woman doesn't hit my car" he snapped. If only he knew who she was! He wanted to talk some more but then remembered he had to call at a shop up the way so he walked off slowly, too slowly for my liking. As he went into the distance, I dived across for Her car – couldn't wait - the top was down, there she was. We kissed. Off she went and just drove. Evidently, we didn't have a clue where we were going, or I didn't anyway. She took me to a pub in the countryside by a canal. We had a drink and a snack and just talked, kissed. Every minute we felt more confident about each other and our relationship. Then we went to a garden centre. Wandering round together was so natural it was if we belonged together as if we were partners looking at plants etc for our home. Then off to a shoe store. All of a sudden, She turned and ushered me away. She had spotted a friend in the store! We managed to dodge around the corner, this

could be a theme, strike two! She dropped me at a park, just around the corner from my relative's. Perhaps that was our naivety or cockiness at doing this. A lot of the things we did without a thought – all we cared about was ourselves. Leaving the park was so hard. "I will text you if I can make it tomorrow" she said.

"Her" - All morning I was anticipating the liaison with Him! Would it be the same now that we were back in the real world? I drove to the shops dead on time! Spotted Him just where he said he'd be and pulled in behind a big car. He was flapping and signalling, something was up! He was talking to someone – Oops! He came dashing over and I drove off conscious that we were nearly spotted by who turned out to be his relative, George. I hadn't a clue where to go, inexperienced in plotting I was trying to think of somewhere nice we could relax and talk some more. I remembered the pub by the canal and headed off; it was just right, quiet and a nice lunch by the water where we could cuddle up. We sat about for a while the talking getting easier every time we meet and then went off to get a few bits from the garden centre – a project together! I'll always look at the plant supports and remember this afternoon! On the way back (I didn't want to say good bye because I didn't know when I would see him again) we called in at a store still looking at sunglasses and for me – always the shoes! A near miss! Alison was looking at the shoes! A quick about turn and a sign to Him and we were out of the store and safety. Time to take Him back to the Park and I was really feeling down because I couldn't see how I was going to get away tomorrow! He had made it clear that he could make his excuses if I could but he wasn't putting any pressure on – I love him! Home again and chatting about tomorrow – The Prof said "You haven't forgotten I'm teaching in Derby tomorrow have you?" Thank you! I was so thrilled! I would be able to see Him again and not worry about time constraints. I still wasn't sure about the text and whether I should call before Saturday so I left it and concentrated on a few jobs at home first! The afternoon couldn't come quickly enough I had arranged to meet Him at the park at 2 PM!

"Him" - Saturday, the text came to life. Andrew was teaching all day. The park at 2pm. I just hope beyond hope that fate keeps helping us. After 40 years without each other we need all the help we can get. Felt a right bozo as I hid in the bushes waiting for Her – just in case somebody came into the park or drove by and spotted me. Paranoid or what! She had bought sushi. This is another reason why I love her. Not because she likes sushi but her thoughtfulness and caring. We sat in the park and shared sushi. We talked, getting quite good at this now. I don't know if it was there but She suddenly brought up the fact that her sex life was virtually none existent now. I sympathized and agreed that I knew how she felt. This was so true, so was mine. It was if we were reading each other's minds, but she had the guts to speak hers. To the phone store, She swapped her phone for a new one and then we went for a drive. I had to put on the radio on to hear a bit of the England football game to complete my alibi. Nobody would believe that I didn't watch the game. Who cares I would rather be with Her. When we drove into the park, just when I thought that I would have to leave her she said "Do you want to go for a walk?", My heart raced, we got out of the car. As I kissed her on the cheek out of the corner of my eye, I spotted a man and his dog, I couldn't believe it, George! – For that split second, I really couldn't believe it! Panic I yelled to Her, George and ran the opposite way. A few seconds later there would have been nowhere to run to and I would have had a lot of explaining to do! I went around to the other side of the little copse and picked Her up on the other side. Our hearts were racing again. Strike 3, by now we should be out, however, this seemed to gel us. We kissed and hugged, I held Her, it was wonderful. Too soon we had to part. I think of the ramifications, but then again think of what I would have missed if She had not have suggested we go for a walk. We looked at her dad's tree, used the new phone to take a picture, it was back to front she ended up with a picture of the two of us. We laughed, this was how it was supposed to be; the two of us in love and enjoying every moment of each other's company.

"Her", I had to shop on Saturday morning so I picked up one or two bits for our lunch. I remembered he had said something about liking Sushi so a couple of wraps and some sushi with a drink took us to a park where we sat on a bench and enjoyed our time together. By this time, I was getting a little sad because I couldn't see where we could go from here, he lives so far away. We walked into the shopping centre and looked at the usual things, clothes, shoes, that sort of thing Then I remembered that I could change my phone, the annual update was long gone! We laughed and chose a phone for me! Time to go again but I couldn't let him go at the park and suggested a walk, just a little more time to hold him and kiss him again! Oops! He dived for the bushes, he said something, I didn't quite catch and I thought "what's he playing at!" A chap with a dog walked out of the park and the penny dropped! His relative George! Had he seen us? I couldn't believe that we had been that lucky but he didn't turn around so I assumed we'd escaped. We laughed and gasped at the experience! We're like 16 - year olds again! No experience! We walked around the park sat on yet another bench, by now our caresses were more urgent and our mouths more exploratory – delicious! I took Him to see Dad's tree and I took a photo of it and one of us with my new toy. I agreed to let Him know by text <u>when</u> I could get away on Sunday, it wasn't a case of <u>if</u> now, I had to make it happen!

"Him" - Sunday, I waited and waited. No text - message. I couldn't expect Her to be able to manipulate her life to suit me and I didn't expect her to. I walked down to the shops by the station with Dennis. Just in case, I briefed him that I might get a phone call from a friend. I was getting very devious, certainly getting the practice. Then it happened. A text. Where are you? "I will be at Boots in 10 Minutes". I told Dennis an old school friend was on his way and sent him on his way. My mind was working overtime. We shopped in Boots. Have not done so much shopping in years. Where do we go next? We are so out of practice at knowing where to go to be together. We both have houses, but when you can't use them were to go? We eventually made it to a small park in the city centre, sat and talked. "I love you" we told each other. – We kissed. If only we could be alone. However, if we managed it, I knew what would happen next! She only had an hour. I was so grateful that she would do this to meet me. She dropped me off at the park. I called in to see another relative on the way back, he dropped took me back and I dozed off as I watched the cricket. George woke me up as he came in, "Did we see you in a blue convertible sports car with a good looking blonde". Oh No! Even though I was still half asleep – I must have lied so much this past few days, I was getting good at it and replied that I didn't think so, "how would I know any good-looking young women with sports cars over here?". I still don't know how close they were and whether they bought my story. Strike 4. Wait until I tell Her about the latest near miss.

"Her" - Sunday wasn't as easy; I had things to do but nothing that could get me away from home! Then I had a brilliant idea, the Prof would need one or two bits and pieces to take in to the hospital on Monday so I volunteered to go to Boots! I texted Him and said I could be at Boots in 10 minutes and he was already on the way to the shops again! We sat in a small park and by now we knew definitely which way we wanted this to go, each touch like fire and each kiss like wine - how could we be together without it seeming too contrived and therefore unromantic? He had business in London on Monday and off back home on Tuesday, it had to be a nice evening for our last contact, this time? Yes, I was sure by now that there would be other times. I arranged to meet him from the train but I had to give some time to the Prof who would have had his op by then. The good old text spoke again and then later we were able to use the phone!

"Him" Monday - I had to go to London. We spoke on the phone when I got there. A long day for me as I left town at 6.40 am. She took Andrew to the hospital for 7 am and was obviously nervous; it was going to be a long day for her as well. I called Her from the office boardroom to check on things before lunch. Tried to stay in touch as much as I could without being a nuisance. When we were chatting in the morning, she mentioned that she had bought some pasta. "Does that mean that you are cooking supper" The first intimation we were going to her house! I hope that she is happy with this – I certainly am – if she changed her mind now, I would be disappointed, however, it is Her who has to feel comfortable. She was at the hospital. "I can pick you up at 6.30 – 6.45 PM" she said. There was no way I could go back to Fred's, what excuse would I have to dream up this time to get out? I waited at the station; it was worth it. Turning up with the hood down I am so lucky to have found her again. I just hope we stay together but I wouldn't do anything that would hurt her or compromise her present situation. "Would you like to come to my house for dinner" she said. I was thrilled. "You don't have to" she said "if it doesn't feel right". I said "whatever you feel comfortable with", hoping she wouldn't change her mind. We were rather uncomfortable to start with in Her house, not like we were in the hotel, or obvious reasons. It was a really nice house with a beautiful garden. Had to be didn't it. It was Her's. She prepared the food; I opened the wine. We embraced and kissed!

"Her" I was able to pick Him up by 6.50 'ish and I was very conscious that he had had to hang around for me after a long day in London. I had bought pasta and wine but still wasn't sure whether He would think it was wrong to come to my house. We could go to a restaurant if he doesn't feel right, I thought! I wanted to see him alone, I wanted to kiss him and hold him for the last time, I wasn't sure that we were ready to make the whole commitment! Well, we were ready but were we going to be brave enough! I drove off towards my home and gave Him the opportunity to say if he wasn't comfortable with my idea. He put the ball back in my court and after a quick panic I thought yes, go for it!

Him" I was worried that she would feel uncomfortable with me in her house. I am sure she did, but our feelings and passion for each other took over. We had dinner in the garden. It was idyllic. We were so relaxed and we talked some more, what a comparison to 40 years ago. If only! We were made for each other. I kept looking at my watch, wishing the world would stop. If there was a point at which you would want the world to seize up and stay in a particular position for ever, this was it. I felt right at home – She was chatting away. I poured the wine and served the salad. What else could we want? Dinner over we talked and talked, the evening started cooling off, we went into the house. We opened another bottle of wine and sat on the couch in the conservatory. We talked we kissed, we embraced we were so close. Caressing each other – this isn't how it was 40 years ago. "I have a spare bed" I needed no second invite. I had never done this before with another woman. But this was my first love. How would I cope, how would I be – I wasn't nervous – the love and the passion for Her had taken over. What would She think or be thinking? We undressed, then straight into bed. It was wonderful. She was wonderful. Why did it have to end? We lay there together and talked again. Why couldn't we have been together longer, after 40 years we deserved it. I should have told Fred that I was staying in London and stayed the night. You only think of these things after the fact. We hadn't a clue that the circumstances and fate would have given us the opportunity. She called me a cab. Half an hour, we talked, caressed and kissed. I don't want to go. She has a life, I have a life, I would change mine in an instant, but I couldn't expect Her to. One day maybe we could be together permanently – but not at the moment, not for now anyway. The Cab came – I kissed Her and literally ran out of her house – couldn't face saying goodbye – I had a tear in my eye as it was – didn't want her to see that. Ciao Bella arrivederci mio amore.

"Her" I was very 'flappy' so nervous I forgot to put the bread in the oven and had to keep the pasta warm until it was ready! He opened the wine and we ate outside, what a perfect night! The meal was good although we probably didn't notice that much of it I'm sure our minds were as one wondering what was for dessert! We sat in the garden until it started to get dusk and we cleared away the debris and sat in the house still talking, touching, kissing……The passion overcame us and I said "there is a spare room!" How brave of me! He didn't need prompting; unconsciously we had waited 40 years for this! We undressed with little embarrassment, the red wine had probably helped that along and everything seemed perfect. The caresses became more ardent and our lovemaking reached its height, we were together in every sense of the word. My lover, yes mine at last. I knew he had to go and we peeled our bodies apart not wanting it to end. I called a cab and they said half an hour; it came before that half hour was up. He rushed off and I could see he was emotional, he didn't want to leave as much as I didn't want to say goodbye to my lover, my first love….

He wasn't with it on the plane going home in fact he was pretty desolate. Sat in his aisle seat in premium economy he wasn't in the mood for conversation, the couple of glasses of red wine didn't really help either. He tried to read, then watch a movie, but they all seemed romantically inclined and he couldn't stand that. Everything that happened, he saw her and heard Dusty Springfield, 'there is always something there to remind me', she was there, in his dreams, he couldn't stop thinking about her as "you are always on my mind" the odd tear came as he heard, 'when will I see you again.' He'd only been on the plane some forty-five minutes; it was getting interminable.

The two guys alongside him were chatting away, not that he was interested in what they were saying, until he heard Mere Folly mentioned. Did he hear right? if he did it was the last thing he expected to hear. Immediately he was paying attention to what they were saying as it wasn't in the context of where they were from. It was more in the context of how they were going to take a look at what's going on there.

As he sat there telling her that he loved her, hoping that subliminally She would get the message, the guys next to him were chatting away.

'Did you read the brief on this place Mere Folly,' said the small skinny guy, as he loosened his tie and pulled a binder from his brief case.

His ears pricked up at the mention of Mere Folly, he looked over and thought who wears a tie on a plane nowadays?

'Indeed, looks a nice little place, seems to have taken off now it's been made a sovereign city state. Mind you that was to be expected especially with all the advantages you can glean from a set up like that.

Archer Finlayson was quite interested to see the place, 'I wonder if these people know what a gold mine they are sitting on.'

It looked as though he had taken the buds out of his ears, but he actually left them there to give the impression that they were inserted. He angled his body away from them, again to give the impression that he had other things on his mind. Forgive me my darling for ignoring you but for the moment business calls, he was all ears.

Finlayson loosened his tie. 'I can't understand why the Government there would set up a scenario like this and have no interest. Evidently, the ex-prime minister was such an arrogant immature prick that he didn't understand what he was doing. Then to cap it all, he lost his job, so if he had any thought of taking advantage of the opportunity, which I doubt, he was sunk.'

Sitting there, pretending to sleep, He was chuckling as he thought to himself that it was a shame the boys couldn't hear this.

Why didn't I think about it sooner?

He pretended to wake up and wriggled about a bit to feign comfort, at the same time pulling his phone out of his pocket, switched on the record app and played around with it. Surreptitiously he placed it on the its armrest table hoping that it would pick up the pair's conversation. Then he closed his eyes to think about his first love while he kept one ear on the conversation going on alongside him.

Finlayson leant across to his colleague, Pearson, who was in the middle of the three seats. 'How serious do you think these people in this Mere Folly place will be about working with its surrounding administration to secede from the country.'

If he was dozing, he wasn't now

'I don't think they know what's going on yet,' said Pearson. 'nobody's bothered to tell them.'

'Yeah, why bother, they will have to follow on once we put this together', added Finlayson

'I don't see why we have been asked to do this,' said Pearson.

Finlayson was in Luxembourg, his friend and partner on a beach in Portugal when they got calls from the foreign office saying that "friends needed a favour".

They both opened their fourth airline issue small bottle of wine, while Finlayson said he could understand why as the people in power in both the seceding administration and the accepting country didn't want their finger prints all over this for the time being. They didn't want any of their key politicians to be seen driving the bus. From what I understand, we are going to talk to these people at this rink dinky place and explain to them that their Sovereign State City is shortly going to be in the middle of a different country and it will be in its own interest to close down its individuality and belong to the country that surrounds it.

There was a gulp as He swallowed hard and made sure that he didn't open his eyes. Hoping that the phone was picking up the conversation and thinking that the boys were going to love this He kept his concentration to remain rooted with his eyes closed in his seat. Keep on drinking the wine he thought, it will keep your mouths moving.

Eventually, He had to go to the washroom, when he got back to his seat, he looked the guys in the eye and smiled. Pearson looked up and made small talk.

'Going home, or on holiday?'

He thought quickly, he didn't want to admit that he was on his way to Mere Folly. That could lead to questions, which presently he would rather not get involved in. 'No, I live locally, where are you off to.' He thought the best form of defence was to attack.

A place called Mere Folly; do you know it?'

'Of course, I live near there,' He lied. 'You guys can't be going there on holiday; I can't imagine it's a big holiday destination.'

'No, we are popping in on business,' joined in Finlayson.

'I didn't realise that Mere Folly was a big business centre.' He was hoping that the alcohol consumed was directly related to the amount of talking they would do. 'What line of business are you in?

There was a moment of silence, Pearson and Finlayson looked at each other. 'Kind of business relations,' said Pearson.

'A rinky dink place like Mere Folly hires business relations people?' He was really getting into it, 'wow it must really want to put itself on the map, I am still trying to figure out what you guys actually do.'

'Good question,' said Finlayson 'but we really can't get into that, you know client privacy, compliance and all that crap.'

Touché, that was it he realised, settled down in his chair, turned the screen on and dangled his ear buds on his ears, as the business relations gurus next to him unscrewed the tops off another bottle of wine.

He looked at the time in London and thought that She would be tucked up in bed. All of a sudden it was driving him nuts, wishing he was tucked up with her.

'You know,' slurred Pearson in between sips of wine, 'how are we going to approach this. I presume that our people will have arranged a meeting. Are we just going to tell them that the country surrounding them would like them to become a part of that country?'

'What if they say no.'

'We tell them that that is not an option.'

He opened an eye and closed it quickly to make sure that the phone was still there. He must have dozed off as he was woken by the noise and movement of attendants wandering the aisles to pick up newspapers and other garbage. As he came to his senses the first thing that occurred to him was to check his phone. The microphone was still working, he clutched it in his hand in case he forgot it in the haste to get off the plane. It was a good job that He took the relations guys seriously as they sat behind him on the puddle jumper going north. Before long they were waiting together at the baggage carousel.

'How long does it take to get to Mere Folly? Asked Finlayson

'I would imagine about forty-five minutes,' He said, 'which knowing this airport is probably the length of time it will take for the bags to show up.'

Then He wandered off giving the impression that he was making a phone call. He was thrilled, the phone had picked up their conversation.

Forty-five minutes later they were still waiting. He now knew that a car was waiting for them, Pearson found the driver with holding a card with Finlayson's name on it, although they still hadn't a clue where they would be staying, such was the rush of getting to Mere Folly.

Eventually, sixty-five minutes after they arrived at the carousel the bags arrived. Finlayson was full of praise for the baggage handlers, 'They must have only taken an hour for their tea break.'

He looked at him and with a gentle smile, 'if it's any consolation at least your bags made it. I hope your meetings go well, perhaps we will meet again in the not too distant future.'

Finlayson and Pearson shook hands with him slightly mystified at his comments and made their way to their waiting car.

CHAPTER 10.

He was shattered and went to bed early but tossed and turned all night thinking about Her and the two business relations guys he met on the plane. He sent her a text and got one back straight away, then he listened to the recording, which really set his mind buzzing. Eventually he did fall asleep again

The boys couldn't wait to get together with Him to hear about his trip. 'Better than I could ever have expected,' he said, 'but, I have far more interesting news.'

'What! You are going to move over there and live with her?'

He was saved by the bell.

'I thought I would find you lot here,' said the EA as wandered to their table in the Vineyard café

'Oh no this is all we need, what now?'

'I have arranged a meeting for you tomorrow morning at City hall.'

'Who with,' asked Bert, 'couldn't you have asked us first if we were free or even wanted to meet whoever he or they are.'

'I think you will want to meet these people; they have flown in to represent their Government.'

'Why would they do that? Why wouldn't they contact us first, not just fly over here. Suppose we were on holiday or on a business trip? We'll get back to you, we need to chat.'

'Ok, but I need to know today, maybe I'll meet with them instead.' He walked out of the café in a bit of a huff'

'This really doesn't make a great deal of sense.'

'It does,'

The others looked up from their cappuccino's and latte's.

'Listen to this.'

He pulled out his phone and started the recording.

'Where did you get this?'

He switched it off; 'these guys were sat next to me on the plane. When they first starting talking about Mere Folly, my ears pricked up.' He switched it on again and told them to listen, they might learn something. After a number of fast forwarding's, replay's and gasps there was no hesitation in telling the EA that the board of Mere Folly would make itself available to meet Her Majesty's Government's representatives.

'The leading question of course is, should I attend. They will recognise me, which could at this time jeopardise things.'

The consensus was that He should not attend. What they wanted to find out was the representatives' story and how it compared to what they had heard from the recording. They realised that they had a decision to make, but it all hinged on what they were going to get out of it. Already there were alternatives: Join the big country, stay with the existing country or stay independent from either of them. Perhaps there was another one.

'What real value we are to either country is a matter of opinion,' said Tom, 'however it will be fun playing one off against the other, if it comes to that.'

Bert was looking worried, 'That's fine saying that but perhaps we should look at it from the opposite perspective, it's not necessarily what is the best deal we are going to get from choosing a particular way to go, but if we choose and go in a specific direction, are we going to be made to suffer? Let's face it, either the potential new country or the existing country or perhaps both are going to lose out and we could be the chopped liver in the sandwich.'

'Before we discuss this any further, what are you going to do?' as the three of them looked at straight at Him.

He looked at his cappuccino.

'The answer's not in there, there aren't even any tea leaves to give you a clue.'

'For the moment she's there, I'm here. I can't see either of us moving to each other's space, so this is my number one priority. I miss her tremendously, but on thinking about it we both have lives where we live. If we decided to live together, we would love it, but one of us would have to sacrifice and miss their existing life, therefore for the time being it will be a long-distance romance.'

The boys asked the EA to confirm the meeting. They were looking forward to hearing what Finlayson and Pearson had to say and as they didn't have to make an immediate decision, they were relaxed and would play dumb which was right up their street. Three of the boys introduced themselves to Finlayson and Pearson and apologised for the fact that the other member of the board was unavailable at such short notice. A subtle hint expressing their surprise at the way the meeting was convened. The EA was rather ticked off as he wasn't allowed to stay due to the fact that he wasn't a board member. The Government representatives explained in no uncertain terms that this meeting was strictly confidential and only the board of Mere Folly could attend. Of course, the boys were pleased that this was requested as they would have told the EA that he couldn't attend anyway as they still didn't trust him.

'You never know what may come out of his mouth when him and Mary Moron are having one of their sessions.'

Finlayson opened the meeting saying that his Government had it on good authority that the jurisdiction surrounding Mere Folly was going to secede from its present country and become part of the country to its immediate south. The boys maintained an aura of status quo, they didn't want these people knowing how shocked they were.

'You don't appear particularly surprised or bothered,' said Pearson.

'Let's say that we had heard rumblings.'

'If this switch of allegiance goes through you guys could be squeezed if you remain as you are. The way we see it, you have a number of options: go back to your present country, go to the country to the south, go back to the surrounding jurisdiction and move south.

'What if we are happy remaining as the sovereign city state of Mere Folly?'

'You have every right but you don't need us to tell you that there will be a rather bitter sweet relationship between your two closest neighbours and you could end up in the middle of the spat.

'Yes, but they might want to fight over us and gives us benefits to side with us.'

Finlayson was quick to jump in, 'True, but then again they might try to squeeze you out of sheer spite. After all you will just be an insignificant entity with no importance what so ever. In fact, you will just be a blot on the landscape to them. How are you going to maintain your city, what about medical facilities, I could ream off tons of items that could cause you distress if you haven't the infrastructure, capital etc. to maintain and keep them going.'

'So, what you are saying is that we should side with one of our neighbours?'

'Not necessarily. We and by that, I mean our Government could look after you if you became a dependant colony.'

'Great, but then we would be subject to your laws and worse still, have to pay your taxes.'

'Not necessarily, are you interested?'

'Let's go to lunch. The washrooms are that way, we will ask the EA to meet you in the lobby and take you to the restaurant.'

A phone call was made to Chat, Claire was primed, they would be sitting at THE table.

'I was under the impression that Mere Folly was just a hick town in the middle of nowhere. 'You've certainly opened our eyes,' said Pearson, 'what a beautiful spot this is.'

'There's lots more that we can show you that will really impress you,' said the EA.

After a quick meal, the boys gave their apologies and said that they had another appointment, but would meet them for dinner. The EA was left, on purpose, to take care of them.'

In between them getting up and leaving, a man with a baseball cap and beard sat at the table at the back and plugged in his ear buds. It was rather dark as He sipped on his beer.

'Nice guys,' said Pearson.

They are.' said the EA, as he took over the conversation. 'Good to have as figureheads and sit on the board.'

'What do you mean?' asked Finlayson.

'Well I was the Mayor of Mere Folly for many years, very well liked even if I do say so myself. At each election I would get in by acclamation.'

Pearson looked at Finlayson and smiled. It hadn't taken them that long to figure out that this guy was an idiot.

'I am responsible for the re vamp of Mere Folly. The guys on the board will do whatever I lead them to say. That's why I had them leave us alone so that we could discuss the reason for your visit.'

He sat listening at the back of the room. The boys are going to love this, when they hear the recording.

There was a reason why Finlayson and Pearson were chosen for this venture. Two of the more experienced operatives. Perhaps not shrewd enough to realise that a few drinks would give them verbal diarrhoea but certainly experienced to know how to recognise and handle an idiot like the ex-Mayor of Mere Folly.

'So why are you here?'

'Good question,' said Finlayson.
Pearson and Finlayson realised quite early on that the EA was not part of the board's inner sanctum. They told the EA that their Government had heard about the development of Mere Folly and they had been asked to pop over, take a look and get some ideas.

This really boosted the EA's ego, he could build a relationship with these guys, go back to the boys and not tell them anything. Down the road he could perhaps work with them secretively.

'Why don't I give you a brief tour and explain what I have done over the past few years to make Mere Folly what it is today.'

'Perfect,' said Pearson as he got the 'do we have to?' look from Finlayson.

As soon as the three of the left the restaurant, He texted the others who within ten minutes were having a beer and listening to the recording.
There was nothing much to learn but at least they knew that the operatives read the EA like a book and of course that the EA still couldn't be trusted.
As they sat at the back of Chat, they still couldn't make their minds up as to which way to go.

'With the various scenarios on the table, I still think that we should review the proposals from each entity, said Tom. 'We know that we are going to get one from Finlayson and Pearson. There will be one from the jurisdiction around us explaining that they are going south. Then there will be one from the Country explaining what it is going to do once the jurisdiction leaves. Of course, we then have to make up our minds as to whether Mere Folly remains independent. The only country that has contacted us has had two representatives fly 9 hours to meet with us. We haven't heard a word from what for the time being is our own country or the jurisdiction surrounding us that is seceding. Therefore, they are really serious and want to work with us, or they are really serious because they have an ulterior motive and there is more to this than meets the eye.'

'Here we go again,' said Jim, 'he's been reading another spy novel.' Let's sit tight and wait for each one of them to come to us with a proposal, we can review and make an informed decision then.'

Bert was still convinced that all was not going to be as easy as the others figured it would be.'

The boys minus one met for dinner at the Vineyard restaurant. Pearson was quite impressed as they were treated like royalty, everybody seemed to know them and they appeared to know everybody. Always guarded as to how much they drank, on occasions like this, they were making sure that their two guests weren't left wanting.

'Let us get this right. You are suggesting that Mere Folly becomes an independent nation protected by your country. If that happens how will it benefit Mere Folly.

The representatives said that they had no authority to provide that information. What they were there for was to make contact with the decision makers in Mere Folly and if there was interest, report back. If the powers that be wished to proceed, a document would be prepared and negotiations begin.

'By the way how did the visit with our EA go?'

'Pretty full of himself, isn't he? We can see you working for him shortly

The boys nearly choked.

The evening passed, dinner a success. '

The four boys reconvened in Chat for a nightcap.

'That's what I like about those two, everything that we heard on the tape was what we were told,' said Jim after the representatives had been parcelled into a cab and sent packing.

"Well I'm for going with these guys, let's face it what benefit would we get from joining the folks down south. Whoever they have leading their country it ends up in a mess."

'I'm not so sure,' said Bert. 'Three of us came here for a better life and we have got it. How can a place nine hours away look after us, it has problems on its own patch. Presently it doesn't know whether it's coming or going.'

'What about our country,' said Tom. 'At least we know and understand it. We have got rid of the idiot that was spoiling and ruining it. Besides we have been presented with a means to rule ourselves by that country. Who's to say that the other Governments will abide by that and treat us fairly.'

'Tom and Bert are right,' joined in Kev. 'At least the country will still have a toe hold in the land that is being cut out of the country to become part of another country that we don't particularly have a lot of respect for. I bet they will want to look after us and protect us and the decision makers aren't nine hours away.'

The consensus had swung, as Bert said, common sense was prevailing. They were happy that they would no longer have to answer to the communist jurisdiction that had seceded to the south.

'I wonder how long that party will go on for,' said Tom.

They had just toasted their decision when the EA walked in and joined them.

He was full of the joys of spring as he explained to the boys that when the deal was done, Finlayson and Pearson were going to suggest that he become the Governor General of the new Independent Protectorate. The boys grinned at each other and suggested that in that case he should follow the three steps to make Mere Folly an independent country or become a protected sovereign state and of course, there would have to be a referendum. They also suggested that he should spend the money to discuss with legal experts to determine whether the way to go was to work with the Government represented by Finlayson and Pearson. They also told him that they were concerned that as ordinary citizens of Mere Folly, the potential Governor General had no previous expertise or experience in governing a country and how was the country going to be protected going forward?

The boys smirked at him as they left through the front door.

As they walked down the side of the building Bert glanced round to see the EA walking quickly across the road. 'Must be on a promise.' He said.

They walked round the building and entered through the back door and sat at their table in the back of Chat.

'What do you make of that?' said Tom.

'Well,' said Jim. 'There's a long list; either he's telling porkies; we mis-read Finlayson and Pearson; they are working behind our backs; he's stupid to believe that we would believe him; that he could run a country, however small; he figures that he will be able to just walk into the job.   That's why I have a gut feeling that those two went behind our backs and tapped up our gullible EA who would believe anything to get into power.'

'I'm not so sure,' said Tom. 'Think about it, we heard their conversation around the table. Unless they contacted the EA late last night or this morning. I reckon he's full of it.'

Bert ordered a round of cappuccino and sambuca, 'Now I am convinced that we have made the right decision to stay with the country that we know, it has provided us with a charter that provides the four of us with the security to govern our sovereign city state. Let's face it they are going to have to look after Mere Folly. It is the only piece of the country left in an area that belonged to it, the final bastion. The last thing that they want is for any other government or jurisdiction to have to the opportunity to put a wedge in the country. Mere Folly will, despite its size, be a buffer.'

'Here's to Mere Folly, proud to remain in the country,' toasted Kev, as they sipped their sambuca.

'So how do we handle Finlayson, Pearson and the EA?' said Jim.

'We don't,' said Tom. 'We just let them get on with it, they will soon find out who their friends are. In the meantime, we can contact our Government, explain to them what is happening and ask how they are going to look after Mere Folly and of course us.'

Kev, with his chair balancing on its two rear legs as he leaned backwards against the wall was deep in thought watching a guy paying a bill on behalf of a group of four.

'You know, it's amazing how much money waiters make. We know how much ours make because we see the books. Have you ever thought how gullible people are when it comes to adding a tip?'

'Come on then, I see words of wisdom ready to be delivered,' said Tom.

'No think about it, look at that guy, now he's no different to the rest of us. The bill comes, most people don't even look at it or for that matter even check it.'

All of a sudden there was an interest in what Kev was saying.

'The bill comes, the card is pulled out and stuck in the machine. A couple of buttons are pressed and then we are confronted by rows of numbered and % signs. Then most of us take a heavy breath as we realise the tip numbers start at 18, remember when 10 per cent was the accepted tip. Not only has that gone up by eighty per cent but also the cost of the food, wine, beer etc. has risen substantially. As an example, look when this place first opened and we first started coming here before we took it over. They had a happy hour with beer, wine and food at lower prices to attract the four till six crowd. Then what happens? Once the clientele was built up the prices rose literally monthly, so impression that happy hour provided low prices became a myth. Then, what to do next to gouge the customer? As most people are having lower cost meals or skipping wine so that they can afford the tip.

'You're a tight fisted pillock,' said Bert, 'they have to make a living.'

Kev looked down his nose at Bert.'

That proves my point, you are one of the herd, you've got more money than sense. They have just been given a substantial increase in wages; our benevolent government has increased the minimum wage. I bet those clowns in the government haven't a clue as to how much they make. So how do you base your tips? Press the 18, 20 or even 25 per cent button without any thought.'

The boys all looked rather guilty.

Think about it, the three-hundred-dollar bill comes. So, you give the minimum tip on the machine, fifty-four bucks. Not bad for an average of an hour and a half's work. Now I know you have to split it, so you are looking after six tables, and you have to split it amongst four people. It still works out at fifty-four bucks an hour plus your minimum wage. Not bad.

Then your bill includes tax so you don't get any value or benefit from tax but you are still tipping on it, boys we are nuts.'

As Kev carried on with his rant, the more the boys' eyes were opening.

Over there the waiter is delivering a bottle of wine, that customer will be tipping based on the bottle of wine.

'Here we go again,' smirked Jim.

'Think about it, it takes the same amount of work, effort, call it what you like, why then does the customer tip nine dollars on a fifty-dollar bottle and eighteen dollars on a hundred-dollar bottle? The same goes for the food there is no difference in effort required to deliver a twelve-dollar plate of pasta or a thirty-dollar steak. The effort, smile etc. involved in delivering it is exactly the same. The minimum wage is not based on the value of the food you provide.
So why don't we crunch the numbers increase the cost of the food by a standard dollar amount and tell the customers they don't have to tip as service is included

'Yes, that's good,' said Jim but you will always get the odd person who won't want to tip for some reason or another and want his or her money back. Then you are putting the prices up no matter that it provides better value, you are putting the prices up and that will go down like water being flushed down the toilet and talking about flushing stuff down the toilet. That's where our money will go if we start disturbing the status quo. Haven't we got enough on our plates without trying to re vamp the restaurant industry. Let's just watch, if the customers have got so much money, they like to throw it away then so be it. Perhaps it is a fair system after all, nobody is forcing you to even give a tip, you can still tip whatever you like, although the establishment is subconsciously making the customers feel guilty if they don't go along with their suggestions, thus driving them to over tip.'

CHAPTER 11.

'Phew, it's a bit bloody cool,' grumbled Jim, 'not many people skating on the river tonight.' The boys were leaving City Hall by the back door, it was minus twenty out there.

'Look at those kids,' said Tom, 'and that little one, boy can he move and it's not the best surface in the world. Oh no is he alright?
'The little kid lost his edge,' said Kev. 'Looking at those skates I don't think that they've ever seen a sharpening blade.'

The boys helped little Adam out of the snow bank and sat him on a bench by the footpath. 'He's moving, looks a bit shaken up, see he's smiling.'

'Here,' shouted Jim, 'you guys get your skates off and give him a hand, help him inside, lie him on the couch.'

As the kids were about to get Adam's skates off a loud voice from the darkness asked them what they were up to. 'Get those skates off the couch.' Yelled the security guy.

The boys took no notice, eventually Kev wandered over to him.

'What do you think you lot are up to,'

'We are trying to help an injured kid,' said Kev
'I don't care what he is, tell him to get his skates off the couch.'

By this time, Kev had had enough. 'You heartless bastard, what's your name?'

'You lot out.'

So as not to upset the kids, Tom was on his mobile and walked over to where Kev and the guard were.

'Phone your office,' demanded Kev, losing patience.

'Piss off, who do you think you are.' said the guard.

Just then, as the police building was only around the corner, flashing lights from a police car appeared outside the front door.'

The guard was straight at the police telling them to throw out the boys and kids. However, he was shocked as the policeman handcuffed him and told him to shut up and marched him to the car. The other cop came back and asked if the kids were ok.

'They are fine, we will get them some hot chocolate from the kitchen.

The kids, all six of them, sat on the couches in the foyer of City Hall, drinking hot chocolate and not quite believing what was happening.

'So, what teams do you guys play for?' asked Jim

'We don't,' said the little guy.

'Why not?' said Jim, 'you all looked pretty good out there.'

'None of us have played in a team,' said his brother carrying his skates.

Tom was a bit confused, 'Who taught you to skate like that then?'

'The TV. We watch the moves and then try them out.'

'What happens when the ice melts?'

'Well we sneak into the arenas until we get thrown out.'

'Thrown out, well I suppose they need the ice if teams are booked to play.'

'No, they just don't like us playing on their ice.'

'Yeah,' said Adam, 'the ice is empty, we couldn't get on if teams were playing or practicing.'

That really upset the boys 'More chocolate?'.

Mere Folly hockey had a reputation within the hockey fraternity for a bullying culture and poor sportsmanship, it was known there that money talked, you had to have money or go into debt if you wanted your kid or kids to play and even more if your kid was good enough or you really wanted him or her to play in a top team. A culture of entitlement had developed amongst the hockey fraternity, many of the hockey parents there thought that their kid was the next coming of Gretzky and pushed them to win at all costs. When playing in Mere Folly people would drop their kids off as they couldn't bear to sit watching Mere Folly parents, fathers and mothers, screaming at the other players, the referees and worst of all their own kids if they didn't weren't doing too well. Giving a hard time to the young referees, opposing players, their coaches and parents had developed over the years, it was like a virus that had become an epidemic.

The boys loved hockey, especially the professional stuff on TV and of course the grass roots level in the local arenas. They had all been to the odd local game, seen the culture in action and wondered about the mentality of a lot of the parents.

'How would you like to play in a team?' said Bert.

'Mum hasn't got the money,' said the oldest of the lads

Kev, was still upset. How has the game of hockey, that was played on the ponds of our country, become such an elitist sport. That's rhetorical he thought to himself, knowing full well the answer.

'How about it if we formed a team?' asked Jim
'Do you know hockey? have you ever played?'
'No,' said Bert.
'Oh, that's great, that's all we need,' said Kyle.
Then Kev chipped in, 'But we do have money. What if we helped you?'
'You would?"
'Have you any friends who like to play but can't?'
Yes a few, but they are not very good skaters.'
Well where do they play hockey now?'
In the basement, we all play mini sticks.'
'Right, we want you here tomorrow night with a parent at 7, ok.'
'Suppose they won't let us in?'
'Don't worry we will be here to let you in and we will have the police here to help us,'

The boys had the city's marketing team working all next to day to organize a package for the kids. During the afternoon, Linda, one of the marketing team phoned Tom.

'We are having some problems,'
'What's up?' said Tom.
'I phoned up the local hockey association to discuss the project and was left sorely disappointed.'
'You know what the guy told me? Our kids would bring down the quality of the other teams and we would have to find somewhere else to play.'
'That doesn't surprise me knowing the mentality of the Mere Folly Bloc as they are known. No wonder teams hate playing in Mere Folly.

Around seven the next night 19 boys and 3 girls had made their way there, but only about 5 parents.

At first the kids shied away when they saw a cop at the back door. The constable wandered along the footpath encouraging the kids to enter City Hall, where there was hot chocolate and cookies waiting.

'Hi Adam where's your mum?'

'She had to work and besides that she wouldn't believe us.'

Once the first batch of kids made it in others quickly followed. Over by a table in the middle of the foyer was a table set up. Each kid was given a hockey puck and a couple of guys from the local sports store were there to size them up for a free brand-new hockey stick. The kids couldn't quite believe it. Each kid was given a folder by Constable Tony with information for their parents. He introduced himself as their new coach and to a couple of other guys he knew who were going to assist.

'How many of you thought that you would be playing in a team with three coaches and a team manager. Let me introduce you to Linda, your team manager.'

Applause rang out and amongst the applause there were tears.

The day after that, one of the arenas had its ice reserved for two hours at 5pm every day for the new team. Every kid turned up, the team manager took down notes as their skates were inspected and what equipment was needed. Eventually they were let loose on the ice, with pucks and skaters everywhere, these kids had never been party to anything like this.

Next day, a letter arrived at City Hall from the Mere Folly Hockey Association effectively banning the kids from playing with any players of their association and using Mere Folly ice.

The coaches were chatting in the changing room while the kids were getting dressed. They should have known better with all the flapping ears but they got carried away. 'It's strange, the senior Mere Folly team always starts off well, it looks good, but never quite makes it. The team always seems a couple of good players light'

'That's because they are said Troy the eldest of the kids.

'What do you mean?' asked Tony.

You only have to hang around our school, everybody knows that if you have enough money your kid can get in the team. Look at the really good players that leave them at the end of every year. He's right said one of the fathers. We were watching the try outs, how is it the best player on the ice never made it? I heard that his parents had just split up and when it came to paying the fees plus the coach's fee, the father lost it with the coach and the coach cut him. The coach makes sure that the players being turfed can't all go to one team. They are good players and a team could be built round them so they all end up in different teams to balance it out and to make sure that Mere Folly doesn't suffer.

This doesn't make sense said Tony, 'just because their faces don't fit with the coach, or for that matter the coach doesn't like a parent.'

'That's part of it, but it's mainly because they have to keep spaces for those kids whose parents can buy them a spot and pay off the coach. That's why none of these kids will ever get the chance to play for

Mere Folly at the top level, no matter how good they are.'

'Why is it you have never said anything?'

'I tried but nobody listened, nobody cared especially when I have four boys and can't afford to enrol them in hockey. The players in the team are all there because their parents just pay up because they all think that their kid will be signing the big contract and don't want to interfere or spoil the ride. The guys helping out just looked at each other; they were all relatively new to Mere Folly and with no kids of hockey age hadn't had the opportunity to get involved in the culture

The coaches were concerned, but Al and Dennis smiled at each other and sensed another opportunity.

The boys were so upset and ashamed at what had been brought up regarding elitism in Mere Folly sport that they called a special meeting of its assembly.

'I wonder how many kids in Mere Folly are affected?' asked Bert and what an insult this is to the many citizens who volunteer their time and effort, in fact it probably costs them money to volunteer, look after and help our kids. We have to sit down right now and tackle this.

The story was carried in the next edition of the newspaper. Courtesy of the boys, it explained how the city being a very wealthy sovereign city state, had declared that going forward Mere Folly will subsidize all sport. The children and youth will play sport for free with the cost of the equipment required and the facilities needed will be met by the sovereign city state of Mere Folly through the education system.

As all sports associations in Mere Folly are presently members of the jurisdiction that has recently seceded to another country it is no longer permissible for them to operate in the City and will be disbanded. Sport will be supported and funded through the education system coaches, trainers etc. will be employees of the City, and act as an umbrella over Mere Folly sport. Participation, equipment and facilities will be free to our citizens, there will be no more unpaid volunteers or autocratic, oppressive controlled organizations. The special edition went on to explain the revolutionary changes and a photo of Tony, the new Director of sport.

The hockey bloc appealed and complained, nobody backed them up as hockey in Mere Folly was under new management and it seemed the easy way to get rid of the debris. It was timed to coincide with the small gap marking the end of the winter sports season and the start of the main summer sports. It was initially rather disruptive but gradually momentum gathered, the various associations were stabilised and the kids loved being able to participate. Everybody had similar equipment with no discrimination.

The cream was starting to rise and would eventually come to the top. The foreign country now surrounding Mere Folly had no issues with them competing with its players and teams. When it came to regional championships Mere Folly sport had to compete within its own country. Day to day league games took place within the school system. Age group select teams made up the various Mere Folly teams to compete in regional and national tournaments. The regional travel was excessive but with its new airport linking it to the main airport hubs it became quite the facility especially with fares being paid by the city.

Al and Dennis wasted no time and were quickly in contact with and upsetting the hockey bloc, elitism was on its way out. Of course, the bloc in its arrogance was no match for Al and Dennis. They had sorted out the soccer association and hung that board out to dry. It was bad enough paying hush money but when they found out that the soccer association was no more, their business on the side gone they were demoralized

Of course, the senior team hockey coaches had a nice little number going which they thought would carry on. At that time the investigators weren't about to let them know that their money maker was about to come to an end. Al and Dennis took a deposit to keep a lid on their crooked operation shortly before the winding up of the various associations was announced. The key figures in the hockey bloc were none too pleased when they found out that in their minds' that they had paid hush money for nothing but as Al and Dennis reminded them that if it got out what they had been up to then what they had paid and were about to pay was a small price for freedom.

The boys were at their table one evening, 'look who's just walked in, it's that guy, the guy who was coaching Mere Folly's AAA midget team and a couple of his henchmen from the association.' Tom nipped to the bar and waived to Claire. She got the message; they were shown to THE table. In went the ear plugs.

Nothing interesting was said for at least fifteen minutes but then they started going on about a league just for elite players. They were talking about what they would charge and how much they would make on equipment and the arenas after the back handers to the arena managers

We will sit tight and wait for this so-called system to expire. The kids will get fed up just playing for their schools and not a series of play offs with the chance of a national championship.

The plan was to disrupt the new program they knew who they thought were the top players they would entice them with money to play in the towns and cities outside of Mere Folly.

'Bit dishonest that isn't it?'

'Who cares,' what a dumb question thought the coach. 'Once the kids get some sense of success we can then go after the parents for money. Kids will pressurize them to get on or keep them on the program. All the teams will be AA or AAA, we will up the fees so that we are all taken care of. Then once we get lots of kids really involved, we will get the sponsorship money just like we did before.'

Leaning back in his chair, with his hands behind his head, the oldest of the five, was concerned. 'That's all well and good telling us how we are going to make money again, but before we didn't have to give a chunk of it to the cops.'

'Let's just tell the cops what their own people are doing,' said little Alex

'Great, but then we would be dead in the water if any of this got out.'

The boys down at the other end of the room sipped their beer and smiled

'Why don't we just send an anonymous letter?'

'Saying what? Read my lips, if details of our scam gets out where does that leave us?'

'No names etc. just plain and simple, that some of their officers are blackmailing people.'

'That makes sense Alex,' Dave carried on, 'think about it, there's no chance of anything getting out, but it will scare the two cops who blackmail us shitless.'

The boys were eagerly listening and getting concerned. 'What if they find I out about the cops deal with the soccer?'

'But the soccer association is dead,' said Jim.

'That's true, but there's always someone around to talk,' added Kev.

Al and Dennis again wasted no time once they had the tipped them off

The hockey guys were told in no uncertain terms that they could play around and send letters but there would be a ditch waiting for them.

'Remember, we know what you are doing before you do it.'

Al and Dennis left, the five of them sat in the cold meeting room of the arena shell shocked and wondering how they found out.

A few days later, Tom and Kev were telling Al and Dennis that enough was enough

They were getting greedy and should get out before something really leaked.

Al and Dennis were suddenly not around, transfers within the force were an occupational hazard of the job they knew that and after a couple of years getting a comfort zone and gaining the understanding of a community, the powers thought it a good idea to move their officers on and let them start and integrate all over again. Perhaps this philosophy was not as stupid as it appeared, perhaps the hierarchy had come across an Al and Dennis type scam before and didn't want to have to clear up the mess. Fate had intervened at an opportune time for them and they disappeared to pastures new.

The hockey guys couldn't believe, the good news, they were in the clear no more hush money to pay and could push on with their scam.

Tony the sports director met the boys at Chat. He had heard that the reprobates from the defunct association were having words with some of the parents telling them that their kid had a better chance of making it by playing outside of Mere Folly and play in in the association that they were putting together.

'Are many taking the bait?' Asked Bert

'Hard to say, it all depends on the parents; they have to foot the bill.'

What about a transfer tax or something like that. Any kid picked up by a team outside of the country, which they are, would be subject to a tax. Kids going to a legitimate foreign university or college would be exempt.

'Great idea,' said Tony, ' can I have the pleasure of breaking the news to them?'

The hockey guys arranged a meeting with the Mere Folly sports council. They thought that with their experience and as they told Tony and his colleagues that they were the best and most qualified hockey coaches around. They told the sports council that they would make Mere Folly the best hockey town in the country.

'That's great, said Tony but we heard that you had already set up an association across the border.'

'That's bullshit, where did you get that from?'

'Just something we heard. So, you want to set up here?'

'Not only set up but run hockey here, cause that's what we do.'

Tony gulped, but was diplomatic and went along with them.' Let me have your business plan for us to consider?'

'Business plan, you have to be kidding, we don't need a business plan, hockey is what we do. You need us.'

Tony went on to explain that they might not need one but the care of the kids was critical so they wanted to see their plans on how they were going look after and nurture the kids, their development and of course understand the financial aspect.'

'Let us have it within the next two weeks, then we can review and see if we can push on.' They got up shook hands and left, trying hard not to laugh as the hockey guys sat there dumbfounded.

One of Tony's colleagues burst out laughing. 'Did you see their faces? They honestly thought that they were just going to walk in and take over.'

As Bert said when Tony told the boys afterwards, 'no fffffin way.'

'Let's sit tight, I just want to see their financial projections, especially where the money comes from. It will be interesting to see how they describe and phrase scam and backhanders, that's what will give us a real laugh,' smiled Jim

The boys were sat at the back waiting and listening as five guys gradually arrived one by on and sat round the table.

The guy doing most of the talking, isn't he the coach who was in the with meeting Tony? I'm sure he is. Yes, you can tell by the way he's not too happy that they have to present a business plan.'

'Not too happy' was an understatement, he called Tony a jumped-up bureaucrat who knew nothing about sport. 'No bloody way are we going to go about wasting our time doing a business plan, don't they know who we are?'

'Obviously not said Kev

One of the other guys said that they should forget about Mere Folly and carry on across the border and just take the good players.

'Look at the setup we built, we've done it once and made money, we will just have to start rebuilding it and make even more for ourselves.'

The boys chuckled, ' trouble is,' said Kev, 'we wouldn't let you get that far.'

The coach was ranting on about how he knew the key people in Mere Folly and he would be having words because hockey there under the new system would be a social sport and the kids wouldn't get the chance to play at a higher level

'And you wouldn't get the chance to deceive and cheat the players and parents added Jim as he put his empty glass on the table and smiled.

CHAPTER 12.

Nothing much was said to the EA, the boys slipped away to meet the PM and his advisors, where they were treated like royalty. The PM wanted to announce that Mere Folly was remaining in the country as a means to illustrate strength and unity after losing the rest of the jurisdiction to the country to the south. However, the boys insisted that there would be time to announce that with an even bigger fanfare once the other parties interested in Mere Folly had been advised.

'Why would you do that?' asked the PM, they nailed us, let's really hurt them.

As they left Bert left with a parting shot, 'you are forgetting one thing, we are happy to remain, but on our terms. Going forward, we are not going to shoot ourselves in the proverbial. They are still our neighbours, we want to live, work and do business with them.'

Now that the boys had a comfort zone and the backing of the country's government, arriving back in Mere Folly, they set to work on planning what they would do next, comfortable in the position of receiving all the benefits that any city and citizen in the country would receive and perhaps even more. In addition, complete autonomy as a sovereign city state.

Round the table in Chat, the board was discussing who to tell first, when the EA arrived.

'Thought I would find you lot here.'
'Arrogant prick ', muttered Tom
'What was that,' said the EA straining to hear
'Another trick,' smiled Tom.
'I don't get it,' said a puzzled EA

'It's doesn't matter now,' said Tom, 'what do you want?'

'This came by courier.' He put a package on the table, everybody could see that it had been sent by the Government represented by Finlayson and Pearson.

'Aren't you going to open it?'

'All in good time,' said Kev. 'Now be a good man, clear off and let us get on with our lunch.'

The EA didn't know where to put himself. He froze, then if looks could kill he stared at them, turned and left. Have they got a shock coming to them when my friends take over? 'I can wait, I can wait', he muttered as he nearly walked through a waitress and out the door.

'Bit harsh Kev, but I loved it, has he got a shock coming to him.' Said Jim.

Bert opened the package. Inside an official looking letter with an embossed crest on it. He stared at it.

'Aren't you going to open it?' Jim asked politely.

'I should just pitch it.'

The letter started with the usual bureaucratic preamble and went on to state that it was prepared to open negotiations with respect to making Mere Folly an Independent Protectorate.

'That's good of them,' said Tom. 'How do we handle it and respond?

'You are good at that stuff Tom; you compose a response and tell them, no thanks.' Said Jim.

'I've a better idea,' said a strangely thoughtful Bert. 'Whose job is it to take care of this kind of stuff?'

There was silence.

'Why the EA,'

More silence, then the penny dropped, the boys erupted into laughter.

Next day, the boys contacted the EA, telling him that they wanted a meeting with him. The EA couldn't believe it when he heard what the boys were telling him.

'I resign' he said. It was an immediate knee jerk reaction, as flooding through his mind was the fact that his relationship, ego, new job and most importantly, the icing on his cake, status had crumbled. Just as immediately he realised what he had done, but before he could recant Jim leapt in.

'No problem, leave your keys, fobs and passes on the table and let me get security to escort you off the premises.'

'But I have stuff in my office.'

'Don't worry, we will send it to you,'

'Maybe I have been a bit hasty,' said a paranoid ex EA again realising what he had done.

'With the greatest of respect,' which in Kev's parlance meant, you're an idiot, 'too bad,' as Jim arrived back in the room with two security people.

The door closed as the now ex EA left the room.

'I've never seen a man in such sorrow with his job gone out the window,' smiled Jim.

The boys were tired after the stress of the past few days, but the penny dropped. They were supposed to be retired and stay away from this stress, that's why they had appointed an EA, he was supposed to handle this. They decided to wait and see if the EA had learnt his lesson and had become somewhat humble.

'Perhaps he will come back, apologise and tell his friends' Finlayson and Pearson that Mere Folly was going to be a protected sovereign state of another country.' Well this was what Bert would rather happen. Although he was a prick, they knew how to handle him.'

Or so they thought.

The ex EA stormed into his house. 'What's the matter with you?' his wife said.

'I've had it with those guys, I've told them where they can stick their job.'

He explained his version of why he would not be the Mere Folly Executive Administrator any longer.

Just when he wanted, needed and thought that he would get her support, Mrs. Ex EA suddenly turned a whiter shade of pale. What do you mean? You are no longer the EA of Mere Folly. What about my standing in the community? How could you do this to me? You had better go back and tell them it was a mistake and that you want your job back.'

'No bloody way,' said the ex EA as he went to the fridge, grabbed a beer and walked out on to the deck. How can I get rid of the bitch? He kept saying to himself. Now's the time, now's the time to get the hell out of here and get away from her. Then his mind stopped in full flow. He realised he needed money and a plan.

In the meantime, and unknown to the ex EA, Mrs. Ex EA was on her way to City Hall.

'Hello,' said the receptionist,' your husband left some time ago.'

'It's not him I want to see.' She snarled looking down on her. 'Where do I find the board members?'

'I will check and see if they are still here.'

'Don't bother I will find them myself.' She stormed off towards the board room.

The board room door bounced open, in strode Mrs. Ex EA, 'without me around as first lady of this city, it's standing as a metropolis of class and culture will be greatly diminished if not vanish. Don't you realise that the reason that Mere Folly has such a glowing reputation is solely because of me. Don't you realise that If my husband leaves his position as the leader of this city you are going to lose me and if that happens you lose your greatest asset.'

There was silence, the boys for once in their lives were shell shocked. They didn't really know her, although they knew only too well of her reputation and now realized and understood that everything said about her was true.

'You have to laugh at him, at his age, cavorting with his bimbo, you know the one with illusions of grandeur and he quits his job. I bet she'll drop him like a hot potato, when he tells her.'

'You know?' said a startled Jim.

'Oh, come on, I've been living with door knob for many years'

'Yet you still live with him.'

'Of course, I make his life as miserable as I can.'

'Why hasn't he left you then?'

'He hasn't got the balls has he. Let's face it he probably thinks she's great in bed, but she has the personality of a snake and the intellect of a cockroach,'

'I guess you don't like her?' said Jim

'Even if she wasn't my husband's mistress, I still wouldn't like her. I got to thinking that if she can end up being a councillor then anybody can. Now you guys have come along and have given me this opportunity for which I thank you.'

The boys didn't know whether to laugh or cry, this isn't the melodramatic, snobbish housewife so full of her own importance. Is this woman for real? thought Bert or is she taking the piss?

'I know that sometimes I come across rather different but I don't want him to walk all over me.'

Looking at the boys' faces you could tell what they were thinking.

'You've no need to worry about my loyalty, all I am after is to grind that terd into the ground and bury his bimbo with him'.

'I really guess you don't like her.' said Jim.

Tom, not known for his diplomacy, shocked his colleagues by putting his arm over her shoulder. 'My dear Mrs. Ex EA, thanks for coming to see us.'

The other three sat in amazement; they knew Tom and realized that he wouldn't be going through this charade without an ulterior motive in mind.

She smiled at Tom as he walked her out of the board room and asked the receptionist if she would take Mrs. Ex EA to the lounge, get her a cup of coffee and a cookie and bring her back to the board room.'

Off they went as Tom darted back.

'Quick, we only have a couple of minutes, we need to get her on our side for a short time, just in case the EA tries to do something stupid.'

'Agreed,' said Bert.

'Cultural attaché,' said Kev.

'What,' said Jim.

'Cultural attaché, said Kev, think about it, a grandiose title, with no power, she will love it. It will get her off our backs for the time being and the ex EA will be infuriated.'

The new cultural attaché walked back into the board room, coffee cup in hand.

'Take a seat, Mrs ex EA,' Tom said.

'In view of what your status and what you do for the City, we would like to offer you the position of cultural attaché to the country that Mere Folly will be a sovereign state of. What do you think?'

There was no need to think about this. The title said it all, her mind was racing and buzzing. Wait until everybody hears about this, me, cultural attaché, do I get business cards? I can't wait until I tell my husband.'

'I am sure that he will be as thrilled as you are,' said Jim smiling.

As the board room door closed behind her, Kev burst out laughing. 'We've created a monster. The people of Mere Folly can't stand her, imagine what they will think of her now, once she starts telling everybody about her title. She hasn't got a clue what it means, but one word is foreign and it has culture in it. It's a good job that we don't have to stand for election, we'd never get a vote after this appointment.'

Mrs CA couldn't wait to get home.

Mr. CA couldn't believe it when he heard the news. He felt bad enough after losing his job and a bit worse for wear after drinking three beers in the sunshine on his deck. However, when herself walked in and told him her news, he was absolutely horrified.

Mrs. CA wasn't exactly expecting hugs and kisses, they weren't exactly the huggy kissy type of people, but his response really cemented the fact that she despised him.

'You must be bloody joking.'

That hurt her, but she was now a new person, she had a title.

Mr. CA walked into the downstairs powder room, threw up and didn't hear her pontificating. In his mind, life if it wasn't before was going to be hell.

She was already making it so. The boys, if they hadn't realized it at the time could not have comprehended the misery that they had inflicted on Mr. CA.

It wasn't much longer before the City was awash with the news that a new cultural attaché had been appointed. Mrs. CA was on the phone to Chat to make a reservation for a dinner meeting with three other ladies, she called them friends, but the ladies weren't so sure. 'Yes, a reservation for the cultural attaché tonight at 6 PM for four please.'

'Can you repeat your name said Joanna at Chat.'

'My young lady, look in the dictionary for the words cultural attaché, you might learn something,' and put the phone down.

Mr. CA was woken the next morning by the sound of the garage door banging. Actually, he didn't feel too bad after the day he had had, he sat up thinking he had had a bad dream, but then remembered that it was all true, it was all coming back to him. Firstly, his wife and her new title. Then he had to explain what had happened to Finlayson and Pearson.

He thought that he had better get Finlayson and Pearson out of the way, they were too far away to punch him or even shoot him. Ironically, the conversation went quite well. He told them that he was disgusted, they in turn told him that they were disappointed, but all was not lost as they still thought that there was an opportunity. To Mr. CA's surprise, they suggested that if they don't get the appointment then they would still need a representative in Mere

Folly and who better than him. Who would be a better candidate than the ex-Mayor of Mere Folly as its ambassador to Mere Folly? In their minds, ambassador was a much more diplomatic term than spy.

'You cannot disclose any of this until the appointment is announced, if you do you might disappear one night.' Finlayson said in a monotone sermon.

Mr. CA didn't know whether they were joking, but thought it sensible to heed their warning. He didn't know how long he could keep his mouth shut as she was making his life intolerable.

'What are you doing today?' Or 'What have you been doing today?' Telling him that she was far too important to cook his dinner or clean the house. It was driving him nuts. He was on the phone to Finlayson and or Pearson regularly asking if them if they had any ideas on what he could do to disrupt her or Mere Folly.

He'd had enough, thank goodness he still had the moron.

'This is the only place we talk any more she said as they lay in bed. 'We might as well start living together.'

Mr. CA let his emotions run away with him. The next morning, he couldn't believe that he had been so stupid, telling the Moron that he would leave his wife and go from the frying pan into the fire. It then struck him that it was only a few years ago that he was planning to kill her.

Mrs. CA had cleared off but not before telling him that she was off on some very important business and would expect that the house be clean and tidy when she returned. He swore under his breath and threw the potted plant at the door to the garage, 'that will give her something to do when she gets home. I've had it with the bitch.'

He walked off down to the canal and sat outside Chat, ordered a coffee and brandy and watched the world go by, trying to figure out what to do next. He was alone, he had nobody; the boys had deserted him, his wife was on a different planet and his lover wanted him to live with her. What next; he was even more eager to seek revenge on his ex-employers, he wanted to strangle his wife and there was no way he was going to live with the moron, perhaps he should go back to his plan of a few years ago and get rid of her. Not get rid of her in the literary sense but get rid of her as in bump her off.

A couple of hundred yards away, the boys knew that Mr. CA would do his best to seek revenge. They were trying to figure out a way of finding out what Mr. CA and the moron were planning.

'They both dislike us, he wants revenge and she is just a nasty piece of work and will stop at nothing to become the Mayor or as it is now, the leader of Mere Folly,' said Bert, 'we should give her the charter to read, especially the bit about who runs Mere Folly. Which one of you wants to resign from the board so that the rest of us can appoint her.'

'You know what,' said Jim, 'they are so stupid, I bet if we offered it to them, they would sit at THE table in Chat without asking who made the reservation. To them, it is the place to be seen. They are so arrogant that they would miss the fact that were the centre of attention for all the wrong reasons.'

'Love it,' exclaimed Jim. 'Let's do it.'

'You what,' said Kev.

Jim was on it. 'We need to hear the ex EA and Mary Moron plotting and scheming. Instead of waiting for it to happen, let's make it happen. I'll get Claire to call them separately.'

'But I didn't make a reservation,' said Mr. CA.

'Well I have you down here for 7 PM'

'She said the same to the Moron who said the same as her lover.'

The boys watched Mr. CA arrive from there table in the darkness at the back of the restaurant. Once Claire had sat him with his back to the rear, the boys took their seats and plugged in.

The moron arrived precisely at seven, they never thought to ask each other about why the meeting. They were thrilled that the other would set up this dinner.

Of course, the boys were tuned in and breathed a sigh of relief when the couple hadn't realized that they had been set up.

The moron told Mr. CA that she couldn't stop thinking about them being together permanently, Mr. CA winced and thought to himself he had to figure a way out of this.

The boys winced, looked at each other and laughed.

'I wonder what Mrs. CA will say when she knows,' grimaced Kev.

'We have to get back at those idiots that run Mere Folly,' commanded the moron, 'do you happen to have an idea of how to do it? knowing what you know and what they have done to you,'

All she cared about was getting rid of them so that she could take over.

Mr. CA was on the verge of telling her about his deal with Finlayson and Pearson but deep down he knew that that would be stupid. For once, common sense prevailed, his mind was churning with emotion deeply regretted what should he do. He trusted her about as much as he trusted his wife.

'You are right,' he murmured, 'there has to be a way.' He was trying to put the pressure on the moron so that he didn't do something stupid and inadvertently provide information that could help the moron. Then he had a brain wave, 'why don't we just invent things, I will pass them on to my wife and she in her new position will be unbelievably eager to pass on to her new bosses.

Again, the boys smiled, but not as broadly as the moron.

'Perfect, not only will that help us nail those guys but also drop your wife in it right up to her big fat head.'

'Perfect,' he beamed, but deep down he was even more certain that the moron was a nasty piece of work, there was no way he could trust her, she would stab him in the back next. In fact, she was poison. The stark reality hit him. He was on his own, he couldn't trust his wife or his lover, the beauty was that at least he knew it now, rather than later as one of them or maybe both stabbed him in the back.

The lovers left the restaurant after vowing to work on a bunch of inventive fallacies that Mr. CA could pass on to his wife.

'Come on my darling, we work better in bed.' the moron whispered in his ear, but to her surprise and annoyance, he told her he had a headache and walked away.

CHAPTER 13.

The moron was doing some curative shopping when her mobile went. Had she not gone through the affront of her lover rejecting her the night before, then she probably would have ignored Elliot's call.

'Guess who's in town?'

She was still pondering whether to just press the button, it had been about three months, but that moment had passed.

'Nice to hear your voice again. How are you?'

'Missing you as always,' he squirmed.' Fancy dinner tonight?'

'Why don't you come out to Mere Folly.' Now she did want them to be seen together by the ex EA, this must be fate.

'Better food at my hotel,' said Elliot in that condescending way he had.

'But better sex in my bedroom, my husband's away.'

Hearing that Elliot's dick not his brain leapt into action. 'Can't wait.'

'Chat at 7.' She pressed the button and smiled, already thinking how she could get the EA to the restaurant at around 7. She was still thinking of how she could get the ex EA in Chat as she booked THE table, 'By the way.' she said to the receptionist, 'can you book a table for Mrs. And Mr. CA, it's a surprise for them.' The moron walked over to City Hall and asked the receptionist if she would phone the CA and advise her that her and her husband had been invited to a surprise dinner at Chat a 6-45 PM, but not to let on who had invited them.

Of course, Mrs. CA was all over that, 'this is the kind of perk you get when you are in high places,' she told him. He bit his lip literally, the pain alerted him to think who would invite them to dinner without letting them know. Mrs. and Mr. ex CA were sitting at their table waiting for their host or hosts to turn up. Already Mrs. CA was not happy, as she had been advised that THE table was reserved for others. Exactly at seven Elliot walked in and was led to THE table.

Mr. CA looked at his wife. 'What's he doing in town?'

His question was answered almost immediately as Mary Moron wandered in conspicuously late, smiled as she walked past Mrs. and Mr. CA's table, to THE table where she literally fell into Elliot's arms. After they had kissed, and sat down, it didn't take much to make the Mr. CA realize that he had been conned. The moron smiled at him a glancing smile, but enough to get her message across. His first reaction was to get up and go, then just as quickly it dawned on him that how could he explain to Mrs. CA that this was all a ploy set up by his mistress.

Mrs. CA asked Mr. CA who the moron was having dinner with. 'I don't really know, perhaps a boyfriend.'

'That wouldn't surprise me, she messes around with all sorts. There was actually a rumor that she was messing around with you,' she smiled with that wry, knowing look that women tend to use when they are trying to elicit information, or the truth when they actually know the truth.'

'When are these so-called hosts turning up?'

Then the ex EA had a stroke of genius. 'They aren't,' he said with a stone face looking directly at her.

'They aren't, it was a bit of a ruse on my part to take you to dinner to celebrate your appointment as Cultural Attaché.'

'I didn't think you cared.' She said full of emotion.

'At first I didn't, but I realize that you were appointed on merit.' It was hard to lie as there was no way he believed what he was saying.

The moron glancing across at the CA's table couldn't believe what she was seeing. She expected the CA to get up and storm off, but there they were holding hands and laughing.

All Elliot wanted was to get the moron in the sack. After a couple of bottles of wine between them, the moron had calmed down and was getting pretty eager to get out of the restaurant and enjoy the rest of the evening. She watched Mrs. and Mr. CA leave as Elliot put his hand on her knee, she smiled at him and suggested they should head to somewhere a bit more comfortable.

Once again, it wasn't easy for Mr. CA to sleep, his world was collapsing. In his dreamworld he thought of going to the airport and flying off into the sunshine and oblivion. Eventually, he dragged himself out of bed, with herself long gone, thank goodness he didn't have to face her that morning. Then it occurred to him that he would have to face the Moron; probably better if it were sooner rather than later. He wandered over to the Vineyard not thinking that his new enemies would be there. Kev, Bert and Tom were outside the café having breakfast, he thought about joining them, but thought better of it.

'What are you up to,' shouted Jim as he wandered up beside him. 'Cheer up it might never happen.'

'It already has,' said the ex EA as he walked away from the café.

'What have you been up to now? come on and join us.'

'That's the last thing I need, you clowns having a laugh at my expense.'

Jim grabbed his arm, escorted him to the café, sat him down and grabbed a chair for himself.

'This guy needs cheering up.'

'I'm not surprised,' said Kev. 'Look at the company he keeps.'

'Look, I 'm not in the mood to be insulted, you've fired me, given my wife a title and created a bigger monster than she already was. Then you've antagonised Mary so that she is out seeking revenge on you and wants me to help her and to cap it all she wants us to live together.'

Mr. CA's coffee came, he had a sip and relaxed a little.

Bert chipped in, trying to be sympathetic, 'We can empathize with you in that living with one woman is bad enough but trying to keep two happy must be a nightmare.'

The boys remembered the conversation that they honed in on at Chat. Each one of them was trying to figure out a way to bring up the conversation without giving the game away. They needn't have worried, Mr. CA was feeling more comfortable by the minute, all of a sudden, he had some friends to talk to and felt like he was one of the boys again and eager to join in and chat.

The chit chat carried on, Jim, became the flavour of the month as in the eyes of Mr. CA it was Jim who looked after him and invited him to join them. It was if there were only two people at the table as they monopolised the conversation. The boys left Jim to do all the talking and do what he was good at, asking pointed questions.

'When will you ever learn that that girlfriend of yours is poison. I can remember once upon a time you wanted to do away with her.'

'I did but I hadn't the wherewithal or the guts to do it, so I thought that I would stay with her to make sure I knew what she was up to.'

'That didn't work too well did it?'

'What do you mean?'

'She's always trying to pick somebody up that will further her ambitions. Look at the deadbeat insurance guy from out east.'

'That was just a business relationship.'

'You fell for it again.'

Mr. CA was saddened, he knew that she was having it off with Elliot but didn't want to admit it.'

'Every time he was in town, they shacked up in his hotel room. He wanted her to get him the insurance business and to run the company here, while with the two of them in cahoots in more ways than one, it would make it easier for her to become the leader of Mere Folly. Of course, Elliot's bitten the dust but that hasn't stopped her from following her ambitions.

Mr. CA didn't say a word, he was shell shocked. Jim was doing a masterful job of telling the Mr. CA like it was but staying as his best friend. Then Jim started to take liberties, at which the other three were anxious.

'We didn't want you to leave your position with us, if you want it back you can have it.'

You are ok with that? Go and think about it and how you will tell Finlayson and Pearson that you must sever your relationship with them.'

Mr. CA was again stunned, but maintained his composure.

This is an important position we are offering you. We must have your undivided loyalty and are giving you another chance. If you will take our advice you will maintain your relationship with the moron. We will trust you not to tell her anything, but feed her with as much misinformation as you and we can provide. This is your last chance; you are never going to get another one. Imagine how you felt this morning and how you feel now with this job offer.'

'I don't know what to say.'

'That's your decision, but if you accept it and let us down, you are toast.'

Mr. CA got up shook their hands and strode down the road, a spring in his step not evident when he arrived.

'Jim, at one stage I was ready to strangle you, but that was brilliant.'

'What do you expect from an HTSI,' said Jim as he leant back in his chair, smirked and cast a knowing wink at his friends.

'HTSI?' queried Kev.

'Highly Trained Special Investigator,' responded Bert with the jaded look that comes from having heard the definition a million times before.

Perhaps he will disappear off the radar of Finlayson and Pearson, or conceivably we can let his strategy with them continue. The only information he will leak to the moron will be fabrication, he is now going to use her. Mr. CA and the CA can keep their eyes on each other, which they will enjoy doing. We clearly don't trust any of them, we will just sit in the weeds watching what the enemy is up to. In fact, we can play them all at their game and feed them with misinformation and fake news.'

Tom's phone rang, 'You are kidding, we'll be over.'

'Where did they get my number? what a stupid question I'm losing it. Its's the police.'

The boys looked at him as if to say, that's your problem

'We have been called to the police building.'

'We! what's going on?' asked Kev

I don't know, the cops asked if I could get the board together and come down to their building'

There were three officers waiting in the boardroom as they were shown in. 'Sit down gentlemen please,' said the head cop. 'Before we start,'

Jim who was thinking ahead of the cop interrupted. 'Can't be that bad,' said Jim, 'at least it's better than a cell.'

The cop with a look of exasperation ignored Jim and carried on, 'Before we start, we have to explain the protocol in the event of terrorist attack or unseemly entrance by unauthorized persons.'

'What have you got us involved in Tom?' Jim asked.

Gentlemen this is standard procedure. Tom and Bert knew and understood from their previous meetings at the police building but of course Jim thought it was a joke.

'Ok, ok,' let's get on with it said Bert getting more impatient by the minute.

The boys were dragged through the protocol paying little attention, more eager to find out why they were there.

'We were called today to a house where we found two bodies.'

That suddenly got the boys attention.

The bodies were those of a man and a woman. Mary Moron and Elliot,' the moron and her ex-boyfriend, I thought that they were toast,' interrupted Kev.

'They evidently are now,' said Jim 'What happened.?'

'Can I finish? But to answer your question we don't really know yet. We are waiting for toxicology tests and the post mortem, but what I can tell you and this isn't for public consumption, they were found in bed together.'

'Surprise, surprise, did they have smiles on their faces?'

'Sorry!' Kev couldn't help himself and cracked up. The cops couldn't help themselves either and soon everybody in the room was giggling like school boys.

'Who found them?'

'Her husband.'

'Shit,' said Bert, 'poor guy'

There was silence

When decorum was regained, the head cop thanked them for coming, but in as stern a tone as he could render, he insisted that these details were not to be released.

'You have our word,' said Tom

'I'm not bothered about your word,' said the cop, 'you had better not divulge any of this, we were told from above that we had to inform you. We have done that and if you will let us get on with our investigation, we would appreciate it. When the details are available, we will call you in to discuss how we will release details or whether we even will release details.'

The boys left in bewilderment and headed to Chat for solace.

'Couldn't stand either of them, but I presume that they died happy.'

'Who's going to tell the Mr. CA,' asked Tom, 'it will be interesting to see how the cops handle the release, how can they not say anything, I don't know about him, from what I understand, he could disappear and nobody would give a shit. But her she's a well-known figure around here, she can't just disappear.'

'No,' said Kev 'we are best out of it, but I tell you Mr. CA, once he gets over the shock will be happy, he was ready to bump her off.'

I think we are all thinking the same thing,' said Jim, ' did Mr. CA do It? Or perhaps it was suicide, or a sex thing gone wrong, or did the husband come back and find them at it?

The pressure off for the time being, the boys set about arranging another visit to the capital. Having told the Government what they were prepared to do, with the letter from abroad, they wanted to make sure that they were on the same wavelength as the Government, before presenting their conditions and putting pen to paper.

The PM and the cabinet, after the ignominy of losing a chunk of the country were delighted to see that despite the letter, the boys re eager to meet.

'We have it here in the event that you need it for, should we say negotiation purposes,' grinned Bert

Again, they were treated like royalty with the appropriate benefits flowing. Next day the boys met for discussions, the Government had put together an agenda.

Jim scanned the outline, 'Funny, this is all about what you expect from Mere Folly, I can't see anything that will benefit Mere Folly, haven't you read our presentation? If the most profitable jurisdiction in the country qualified for subsidisation then so should Mere Folly after the risk it was taking to stay in the country.'

The Government wanted to make the decision public and reap the accolades, but the boys insisted that they wanted to do things properly and they certainly weren't happy about the terms that they were being offered. They would contact the other interested parties, advise them of their decision and at the same time and most importantly advise the citizens of Mere Folly that although it was a sovereign city state it would be remaining a protectorate of the country.

'Well if we are going to look after you, the country will want paying for it.'

'We understand that,' interrupted Jim, 'but there's nothing here about the most important issue; equalization payments! If you clowns' think that Mere Folly is going to be like the jurisdiction we are leaving and help subsidise the rest of this country, then you can run your circus without us.'

The boys were visibly upset, stressing that Mere Folly had a number of opportunities to secede and be well looked after financially. Therefore, if the country wanted Mere Folly to remain, it had to look after its sovereign city state. If not, it was back to the drawing board to decide on of the two remaining offers on the table, which one was most beneficial.

'Kev get on that Uber app and let's get to the airport,' said Bert, getting out of his chair. 'After all we have tried to do to work with you lot, we get treated like this.'

'That's ok,' said Tom. 'They are no different to any other politicians, but better we get out now with our virginity intact, before we find out that we have been screwed.'

The boys thought that they might be stopped and were surprised that the politicians just sat there. What they didn't know was that the politicians were stunned and waiting for each other to say something.

Bert led the way, 'well, are we going west east or south?'

'Certainly not home yet, so it's either east or south, we'll phone from the cab and make a decision.'

Again, the boys were somewhat surprised as they left the building and into the waiting cab.'

It was three in the afternoon, 'No good going South,' said Jim, 'they'll be closed when we get there, I'll text Finlayson when we get the flight booked it should catch him before he goes to bed.'

'I feel better now,' said Kev just as flashing lights and three police cars brought the cab to a halt.

'Who are you guys?' asked the Uber driver in a matter of fact sort of way.

'A cop opened the door, 'sorry to barge in like this but the prime minister has asked that you join him for dinner.'

'Me as well?' joked the driver.

'If you want to,' said Tom, 'at least we don't appear to have an option.'

'Think I'll pass said the driver, Wednesday is pizza night at our house, otherwise I would be right with you.'

Bert paid off the driver, 'remember our faces, if you see us on tv as missing persons, you know the PM did it.'

The driver sat there speechless as the cars with their newly acquired passengers on board took off, 'naaah, the wife wouldn't believe me anyway, 'as he drove off to pick up the pizza.

The boys rolled their eyes at each other, they knew enough not to speak. They were dropped off back at the federal building that they had walked out of an hour ago. Two suits put their hands out to welcome them back, the boys ignored them.

'Follow us'', the taller and heavier of the two ordered. His attitude suddenly changed after the rebuke of the boys not accepting his hand of welcome.

Tom let him lead off and then called after him, 'We'll be with you in a minute.'

'We'll wait with you,' said the small tubby guy.

Tom explained to them that they wanted five minutes to chat.

The tubby guy looked up at the boys and told them that they should follow him, with an arrogance that really annoyed them.

'Piss on you,' you said Bert. 'We've had enough of this crap, let's go and find a cab.'

The little guy was on his phone.

'I wouldn't do that sir,' said the big guy.

Jim looked up at him, 'Why are you going to give us a lift to the airport?'

Just then, from out of the covered entrance appeared another well dressed, tall grey-haired lady.

'Gentlemen, we would really like to talk to you, would you follow me.'

'No thanks,' said Kev.

The boys walked away. Twenty yards down the forecourt was a cab. The boys walked toward it. As they were getting in, a tall guy appeared, 'I wouldn't do that sir.'

'Piss off,' said an angry Bert, 'we've had enough of you clowns.'

'The airport please,' said Tom.

As time passed by the boys kept looking around expecting to see flashing lights'

'I don't get it,' said Jim, 'why did they get Mutt and Jeff to escort us. If the PM or one of his ministers had of met us and welcomed us, we would be there now chatting.'

The Prime Minister wasn't as gratuitous as the boys, Mutt and Jeff were fired and escorted out of the building into bureaucratic oblivion. He kept saying to himself over and over again, why didn't he do as he wanted and not listen to those security idiots.

At the airport they looked at the check in counters, glanced up to a long glass window.

'That must be a lounge' said Tom

The boys went straight up the escalator, into the lounge, grabbed a drink, grabbed a seat overlooking the counters, watched and waited.

Sure enough, a bunch of guys came over, talked to the staff, flashed a card or something, moved out away from the crowds, stood around and waited.

'They are in for a long wait,' said Bert, 'although we aren't going to sit here all evening.'

No need said Kev, let's go over to the airport hotel grab a room and leave in the morning

'Love it,' said Jim.

They walked back to the lounge; all the PM's men were still there.

'You would have thought that they would have got the message by now.'

One of them was on his phone, then a few went one way to the door, the others up the escalator.

'I wonder if they will come in here?' said Bert, 'Jim, why don't you and Kev stay here, its best if there aren't four of us sat together. I am sure that they really don't know what we look like, but the only party of four guys sat together could be a bit of a clue.'

Tom put two empty glasses on another table. 'Bert and I will nip to the washroom and if they do come in here, when we come out, we will sit near them to see if we can hear anything.'

Back at the Government offices the prime minister was concerned, mainly because he nor his 'people' knew where the boys were. He was sure that they had not left the capital, but as they appeared totally frustrated, knowing that there were other players, unsure as to whether they had opened negotiations with anybody else.

This was confirmed by a phone call from the airport lounge, as the agent was breaking the news to his boss, he was looking around the lounge. 'They hadn't purchased tickets, or passed through security, it's not exactly busy in here, a man and woman and two guys looking out the window. How could four guys disappear in this place? Perhaps they didn't come in here in the first place. What do you want us to do next?'

'Just hang around,' said his boss.

In the bar of the airport hotel, the boys were also deliberating about what to do next. They wanted to work with the prime minister, not because they liked him but rather that he owed them as they had helped him get into power in the first place. They were dealing with politicians and they wouldn't or didn't trust any of them, he was as good as it was likely to get.

A mobile phone rang, 'What time is it over there? I miss you too, mmmmm love you too, good night.'

The PM was still pacing around. 'If it were you what would you have done, or doing or planning?' We know that they didn't get a plane out of here, it's late at night, what would you?'

'Well,' said Hopkins, sipping on his brandy. 'They could have rented a car, got a cab, got a train, got a bus,'

'No way, it's late at night, knowing those guys, they aren't spring chickens, beer and bed. What about the airport hotel, see if they have checked in there? Come on, I reckon we still have time before they go to bed.'

'You are a legend,' said the patronising Hopkins as he put his phone in his pocket.

'Makes sense,' said the PM the bar and a bed are just a brief walk across the pedway. Book a room and into the bar for a night cap to figure out where they are going tomorrow.'

'Gentlemen!' beamed the PM as he put his hands' on Kev and Jim's shoulders.

'Bloody hell. What are you doing here?' said a shocked Jim rhetorically.

'I got to thinking,' said the PM pulling a chair up and sitting down. 'about you four, it didn't take long to rationalise.'

'With the greatest respect, what do you want?' asked Bert. Obviously, the PM hadn't sought them out in the middle of the night to wish them bon voyage, no, they were going in at half time three goals up.'

'Perhaps we should arrange a meeting room said Hopkins?'

'What's wrong with right here?' asked Jim, 'I've been thrown out of better places than this.'

The PM looked around the bar.

The atmosphere changed. 'Sorry,' said Tom, 'we appreciate you catching up with us, let's get a room and discuss what you have in mind.'

'Your usual tactful approach Tom.' The PM's sarcasm was ignored by Tom, he knew that the PM had to come out of this meeting with something positive and was fully aware that the he was determined not to be taken advantage of.

'That's a bit harsh sir,' Tom carried on in his planned condescending manner.

The nod came that the room was ready

It was 11pm, the PM was tired and in no mood to put up with being patronized and listen to bullshit.

'Look, I'll be brutally honest. The fact of Mere Folly being an island in the middle of a foreign peninsula that splits our country causes us great concern.'

It will be even more problematic for you if Mere Folly were to hitch up with an overseas power or the power to the south, fired back Tom

'You wouldn't?'

'Of course we would, chipped in Bert, you can't

be that stupid not to think that we wouldn't. Obviously, that's why we are here, isn't it? Hold on; you actually think that Mere Folly has definitely made up its mind to stay in the country.'

The PM's face was ashen. 'You mean you are not?'

The boys couldn't believe what they were hearing. They smiled at each other grasping the fact that they had the Government by the balls.

'Actually, said Ken, we were planning to fly off tomorrow evening for meetings with a potential suitor.'

'It's late, said Tom. It's been a long day, let's reconvene in the morning refreshed. You can finalize details of the benefits you feel comfortable in delivering, we can discuss prior to taking our flight.

The boys met early and to a man were still convinced that the sovereign state of Mere Folly protected by their nation was the way to go.

It was a bit subdued as the PM and his team welcomed the boys.

Bert was enjoying the opportunity to be a diplomat, ' Mere Folly would like to be a protectorate of your country.'

The PM and his team smiled.

Off and on they had been working on a list of benefits and conditions which would be used as the basis for negotiation with the various Governments. The document was fine-tuned and finalized by their lawyers, copies were printed and set up in leather portfolio's for presentation.

Bert placed a presentation portfolio on the table. 'Of course, our alliance will be subject to your Government accepting these terms and conditions.'

There's always a smart arse in every meeting and this one was no exception. 'And if we don't?'

The PM didn't say anything, he just stared at the guy; if looks could kill.

Bert also put the smart arse in his place. 'I presume that that question was rhetorical and you already know the answer.'

There was a kind of hush in the room as the PM shared the portfolio with a couple of his colleagues. They thumbed through it, pointing out clauses to each other. 'Interesting, ' said the PM, 'we will need some time to review and respond.'

'We fully understand,' said Tom. 'We are happy to stay another night in the hotel and meet with you in this room tomorrow hear any comments and your decision.'

'You've got to be kidding,' chirped up the smart arse, 'who do you guys think you are?

The PM stepped in to save further embarrassment and agreed that he would review with his team and meet the next day at three PM

'Perfect, we will look forward to it,' said Kev
The room quickly emptied the Government back to town and the boys to the restaurant

'We should think about a plan B and perhaps plan C,' said Jim as he ate his lunch.

'That's easy,' went on Kev, 'we go overseas or south.'

'There's the problem.' Went on Jim. As soon as we approach the other parties, we are at a bit of a disadvantage. We appear as if we are grovelling and leave ourselves wide open to negotiate for a suitor on their terms. We just can't do that.'

Tom was a bit more comfortable, we do have a Plan B, the letter from abroad.'

'What about our friendly Mr. CA?' asked Jim.

After going backwards and forwards discussing as to whether he really did have a relationship with Finlayson and Pearson and whether Finlayson and Pearson will have any clout when the real negotiations start, they felt that they did have a strong Plan B. Nevertheless, Plan C, the country to the south was remote, there had been no contact and besides that did they want to deal with an unstable Government.

They each went off to their individual rooms to catch up on phone calls, messages and a mid-afternoon nap, knowing that for once the ball was in somebody else's court, but they had a plan B and perhaps a plan C. The following day they would know which Country would be Mere Folly's guardian.

There was a message waiting on a particular mobile phone. It was asking if he would give her a call, she was missing him tremendously and wanted to know if he was to visit her or she was to visit him. His stomach was in knots, even though he was used to negotiating, arguing giving good and bad news to significant and key people. This was different, this was about giving bad news to the woman that he loved. His phone rang a couple more times that afternoon. He ignored it, but didn't sleep much at all.

'It was a long night,' said the PM, 'but I think that we can come to a meeting of the minds. We went through your proposal, there are a couple of issues,' and passed out a paper to each of the boys.

'One of your team is missing,' said Jim politely.

'He will no longer be involved,' said the PM. 'He has left the Government's service.'

The boys smiled knowingly, whether the PM was lying to them as politicians do from time to time, they didn't really care, they just wanted to get on with the meeting and force their deal through.

'In essence, the changes are quite minor,' added the PM.

On the surface the boys were happy with that statement, but they had heard that kind of rhetoric before from politicians, it probably meant that they wanted the whole thing re-written. The amendments were sent to their lawyers to get their input.

'While your lawyers are reviewing,' said the PM 'and as a way to show our support and desire to make Mere Folly an inspiration to our country, we have an opportunity for you to emphasize your commitment to our country.'

The boys smiled at each other, their thoughts the same, 'ha ha, the old bribery ploy.'

'Let's hear it then,' said Tom unemotionally.

'There were a number of insurance companies licensed and regulated by the old jurisdiction prior to its separation. Obviously, they had a number of alternatives. Get licensed and be regulated by their new country, which they weren't comfortable with. The regulators down south had had a look at them and contacted us about their financial stability when compared to the quality of their business. This caused the Companies concern knowing that for the considerable future they would be under considerable scrutiny from what they considered to be foreign regulators. Secondly to wind the companies up and thirdly, which they did, to come to us and ask if we would re license them. Our regulators were of the same opinion as those to the south.

The management of each of the Companies was poor. Their underwriters were inexperienced with respect to the business that they were writing. Both of the insurers were being selected against by their brokers. Our auditors were very concerned, as the balance of their books of business were out of whack, with their reinsurers concerned as well it was inevitable that they would be closed down.

'So, what do you want us to do,' said Bert. 'Your auditors seem pretty damning in what they are saying, why not just close them down? It's not your problem, surely that's the problem inherited by the country to the south.

'Bad optics, especially at a time like this,' said one of the PM's team.

'But they now belong and operate in another country,' said Tom.

The PM's expert in this area, Claude, carried on, explaining that if these companies were wound down, the ownership would suffer financially.

'Yes, but the owners directly or indirectly chose to align themselves with a different country, that's their problem.

Claude continued, 'As you are very experienced in this area and have the expertise and other staff with expertise here's an opportunity to consolidate your little Empire.

Tom jumped in, 'that's all well and good but we aren't going to buy three virtually bankrupt and inept insurance companies.'

'We don't expect you to, they will be handed to you to own and operate within your financial umbrella.'

Just then, a number of mobile phones rang virtually simultaneously. One, with a text message from a lady overseas, one, with an e mail from the boys' lawyers, one, from the police and one, from a foreign Government ....

Made in the USA
Monee, IL
07 July 2025